Secrets in Avalon

Book 1: Into the Avalon Forest
By

M'Sharra Peters

Purpose Publishing LLC.

13194 US Highway 301 South

Suite 417

Riverview, Florida 33578

www.PurposePublishing.com

Table of Content

AUTHOR'S NOTE

Dear Readers,

I am super excited that you've decided to join me on an adventure to unlock the secrets in the *Secrets in Avalon* series. As a fan of books, whether fantasy, mystery, or adventure, my dreams of becoming an author, which I've had since I was a little girl, have finally come true. I am beyond thrilled to share this world with you. This book series has been a long time in the making, filled with many habits of my indecision-making. I can't wait for you to dive into the magical, mysterious, and thrilling journey that awaits you in Avalon.

This book series is not just a story but a fulfilled journey. I've used writing to escape life's challenges for years, and it has been my greatest comfort. From struggling to fit in, especially in elementary and middle school, to expressing my creativity, writing became my safe space. This passion grew when I was six years old, and it was through the nostalgic shows, movies, computer games, video games, and my love for books and stories that started my dream to write my own stories one day. After seventeen years of learning and growing as a writer, that dream has finally become a reality.

In *Secrets in Avalon*, you'll follow the Mystic Pact—Hannah Sumpter, a sixteen-year-old girl who moves to Avalon, Missouri, after her sister's disappearance—and her friends Sydney Barnes, Zoey Park, Dominique Guerra-Arias, Amber Dodge, and Nia Washington. Together, they uncover Avalon's hidden world of fairies that coexists alongside their own. As they delve into the magical world, they'll learn that the strange occurrences at their school are linked to something far more sinister than they could ever have imagined. Throughout their adventure, the girls not only uncover the mysteries of Avalon but also the secrets of their pasts. It will also lead them to dark magic, secrecy, and a battle between good and evil.

This series is for anyone who loves fantasy, mystery, and a good adventure. It is for those who believe that the power of friendship, courage, and magic is the key to overcoming challenges and that a person's strength can change the world. The characters in this book series are inspired by those who've shaped my life, from my family to my friends, professors, former teachers, and even myself. Nostalgic shows, books, and movies that shaped my childhood inspired me, such as *Bratz: Fashion Pixiez*, *Winx Club*, and Barbie movies like *Barbie: Fairytopia*, *Barbie Fairytopia: Magic of the Rainbow*, *Barbie: Mariposa and Her Butterfly Fairy Friends*, *Barbie: Thumbelina*, *Barbie and the Magic of Pegasus*, *Barbie: A Fairy Secret*, and *Barbie in the 12 Dancing Princesses*. Blending these with *Nancy Drew*, *Pretty Little Liars*, and encouragement from my creative writing professor, as well as my own experiences growing up in Kansas City, helped me capture my imagination and use these as influences in the world of Avalon.

Even though Avalon is just a fictional city, this serves as a representation of the places I've lived, visited, and loved throughout my life, especially in the Kansas City area. What made me choose Missouri as the perfect setting for this book series is not just my Missouri roots; it helped me think outside of the box since many authors have never used Missouri as their setting.

To anyone from grades 5th–12th, I hope this series encourages you to believe in yourself, strength, and magic, and reminds you that no matter what challenges you face, friendship and courage can see you through the struggles and challenges in your life. Thank you for deciding to go on this incredible adventure and mystery.

Now, let's unlock the secrets and show that magic and friendship come to life!

Sincerely,

M'Sharra Peters

CHAPTER 1

Hannah Sumpter's eyelids felt heavy as her head leaned slightly against the car window. The sleeve of her white feather-print crewneck sweatshirt brushed against the smooth leather of her seat as her dark brown eyes fluttered, sleep tugging at her. Her parents' voices faded with every passing mile as she battled to keep her eyes open, struggling to stay awake. It had been almost ten hours since they left Chicago for Avalon, where her mom was starting her new accounting job.

Her parents assumed Hannah would be excited about being in a new city, but in her mind, she wasn't. Ever since she was little, her older sister, Caroline, disappeared without a trace while playing in the park. Hannah often had nightmares about her and the unknown places that Caroline vanished to. She couldn't even recall or describe any of those places. She'd linger on each memory of her nightmares that she couldn't fully remember, almost like shadowy fragments that refused to escape.

Her mom, Maggie's phone buzzed from her dark red shoulder handbag, the sudden sound pulling Hannah away from her thoughts. Maggie picked it up, and after a moment, a smile spread across her face as the FaceTime video call connected, revealing Hannah's grandmother, Corinne, waving happily on her phone screen.

"Hi, honey, how is the ten-hour drive?" asked Corinne, her voice warm and cheerful.

Maggie let out a long, heavy breath as her shoulders slumped against the seat. "Mom, you have no idea how long that drive was, but we made it!" she said, handing her phone to Hannah's dad, Jeremy, with an excited but tired smile.

While his hands were holding the steering wheel, Hannah's dad glanced at the phone, his eyes flickering briefly to the screen.

"Hi, Corinne!" he replied excitedly.

"Hi, Jeremy," Corinne said warmly. Maggie then turned her phone toward Hannah, who was already asleep, and her eleven-year-old sister, Sadie, who was also fast asleep beside her, snuggled up.

"Looks like Hannah and Sadie slept through the whole drive," Maggie gently laughed.

"I can tell," Corinne chuckled, her tone dropping slightly to an uneasy tone.

"They are going to love their new schools," Maggie continued. Corinne's smile faded, her eyes flickering to the side as the corner of her lip curved across her face.

"I had hoped they could stay at their old school," she murmured. Maggie let out a soft groan as she shook her head a bit. "Not this again," she muttered, rolling her blue eyes.

"Maggie, I'm just saying—" said Corinne when Maggie interrupted her. "Mom, I told you we wanted to make a fresh start," she said, her voice firm but tinged with impatience.

Corinne's brow furrowed, her voice ringing with disbelief. "Yeah, but I never imagined you'd take that new accounting job and move to some strange city ten hours from Chicago," she replied.

Maggie released another long breath, her eyes briefly flickering to Hannah and Sadie before returning to Corinne. "I thought being in a new city was the best solution to all of our problems," she said, her tone softening as she tried to brighten the mood. "Look, I know things haven't been the same since Caroline disappeared, but maybe it might give Hannah and Sadie a chance to make new friends and move past all of this. Plus, I heard that Avalon is the third most popular city and suburb in the Kansas City metro area."

Corinne exhaled deeply as if the weight of her words settled on her shoulders. "Call me when you get there and get settled," she said in a low tone.

Maggie smiled faintly, her lips barely lifting. "Okay, love you," she murmured tenderly.

Maggie ended the call and turned her gaze to the window, lost in her thoughts.

Still half awake, Hannah stared at her drawing of a fairy riding a pegasus, her gaze seemingly drifting as if the picture was almost pulling her drowsy mind from reality. Whenever Caroline's name was mentioned, or she had that same nightmare about her, she would draw pictures to cope with her disappearance and keep her mind focused.

By the time she was in kindergarten, Hannah had developed a talent for drawing. She drew her first picture of Caroline and her playing at their favorite lake beach. Then, when Hannah was seven, she would have strange dreams and nightmares about fairies, sprites, pegasi, and all kinds of mysterious, magical places and objects. Each time one of these nightmares recurred, she would recall them by drawing a specific picture, remembering the details as best as she could.

Jeremy pulled his black Nissan Pathfinder to the driveway, the engine's hum slowly fading as he shifted into park. He and Maggie emerged from the car, their eyes settling on the bungalow house ahead of them. The moving truck workers stood waiting nearby, their voices murmuring as they worked while the truck hummed distantly.

The house was modest yet inviting, painted in soft shades of gray and white, revealing its moderate charm. Its trimmed windows were coated in white as it basked in its afternoon sunlight. A gray vinyl screen door stood before a dark gray door, giving the place a crisp and airy look. A slate-gray wall-mounted mailbox was to the left, next to a charcoal-colored push-button doorbell.

"Hey guys, look," Jeremy said, his voice loud and clear, ringing in the girls' ears.

Hannah pulled her attention away from her sketchbook as she and Sadie stepped out of the car. The family stood together, watching the movers maneuver back and forth, unloading their things from left to right.

"Is this our new house?" asked Sadie, her brown eyes flickering with curiosity.

"Yep, our new house in a new city," said Jeremy, a cheerful smile forming. The girls didn't say a word. Their eyes darted nervously around the house, hesitating at each detail while uncertainty inched onto their faces. Soon after the last mover left, a female real estate agent emerged from the house, her navy-blue toe ballet flats clicking, echoing on the gray sidewalk as she approached them.

"It looks like everything is in place," she said, a cheerful smile forming. Jeremy and Maggie exchanged a look before smiling back at the real estate agent. "Thank you so much. It's perfect," said Maggie.

"Now, if you have any problems or questions, don't hesitate to call," said the real estate agent.

"We'll be just fine. Thank you so much," said Jeremy, nodding his head. Hannah and Sadie watched quietly as their parents and the real estate agent shook hands firmly. The agent handed them four pairs of silver keys before walking away. Sadie turned to Hannah, her eyes wide but clouded with uncertainty and doubt.

"Something tells me we're gonna hate it here," she said, her tone flat and reluctant.

Hannah rolled her eyes before following Sadie as they walked toward their parents. "Couldn't agree with you more," she murmured.

Jeremy turned to the girls, a grin spreading across his face. "All right, girls, here are your house keys. Grab a box, and let's get this dog and pony show started," he said excitedly, tossing each key to Sadie and Hannah.

The entire family walked to the car's trunk, and each grabbed a box. In a single file line, they entered the house, filled with familiar furniture from their old house back in Chicago. The walls were painted in a deep mocha brown, decorated with their family pictures on each wall, and had polished oak floors.

The well-worn cushions of their familiar beige modular couch, which had been in the living room for years, appeared before them as they entered. Its plush, soft fabric brought out the memories of their usual family gatherings. In front of it was their sturdy, rustic, sleek, light brown industrial coffee table. Across the room, their espresso brown console TV stand stood beneath the wall, holding their favorite DVR. However, it was the black TV screen that caught their attention. Its oversized and glistening feature stretched across a large portion of the wall.

White walls naturally flowed into the eat-in kitchen, blending the two areas effortlessly. A beautiful marble countertop extended across the room, letting its smooth surface acquire the light while it differed from the modern black faux marble dining table. Their parents, smiling with delight, complimented how the countertop and the table added a touch of sophistication.

Hannah and Sadie exchanged a look, finding its elegant and classy appearance less appealing to their taste. The dining room also featured two doors: one leading to the living room and the other back to the hallways, with a straight staircase and a gray screen door opening to the patio.

"Okay, I think I'm gonna like it here," said Sadie, her voice lifting with a hint of excitement, though carrying a hint of sarcasm.

"See, I knew you would like it," Maggie replied cheerfully. "All right, let's get to it."

As she and Jeremy started moving toward the house, Hannah and Sadie exchanged a look with each other.

"Just so you know, I call dibs on the first room," Sadie said, still carrying the box labeled "Sadie's belongings" in her arms, her pace quickening.

Hannah didn't even care at this point. She grabbed a box labeled "Hannah's belongings." She reached the top of the stairs and opened the gray door to her new bedroom. Setting her box by the door, she paused as she was taken in by her surroundings. The room was airy and flooded with natural light. The walls were painted mint green, giving the room a calming, fresh tone. On the far side of the room, her ivory storage bed frame stood beneath its ivory button-tufted headboard, completed by her plush mint comforter and white pillows peeking out from her spring green pillow covers.

Hannah noticed her ivory double dresser against one wall. The closet, with its white pocket door, revealed a large but vacant space where she could perfectly put her clothes and shoes. Her ivory computer desk stood nearby, accompanied by her green gooseneck lamp. She let out a weary sigh and placed her box on her bed, starting to unpack. She folded her clothes neatly and arranged them in the dresser, then placed some of them, along with her shoes, in the closet. Her accessories went on top of the dresser, and she put her toiletries in her new bathroom. After setting up her bedroom and bathroom, she put her hand-drawn sketches of fairies, pegasi, and sprites on each area of the wall.

A sense of calm filled the space as the day turned to dusk. Everyone was getting a new, refreshing feeling with their new house. Hannah lay in bed, staring at a video on her old sage-green instant camera that she had when she was younger. Her green portable speaker played one of her favorite songs, "Faded" by Everlife.

In the video, Hannah, just two years old at the time, laughed as she and Caroline, just four years old, splashed beside her at the Sea Shore Water Park Resort in Chicago. Still a baby, Sadie kicked her feet in the shallow pool, splashing beside Maggie. Unexpectedly, Jeremy appeared out of nowhere, catching Hannah and Caroline by surprise. They squealed in delight as he hugged them tight, their laughter filling the air. Hannah briefly closed her eyes as her mind drifted back to the carefree days when she, Caroline, and Sadie were always together. It felt like everything had changed since Caroline's disappearance. Since then, Hannah and Caroline had grown even closer, becoming inseparable. They always had each other's backs, especially when it came to protecting Sadie. Hannah and Caroline were more than just sisters—they were best friends. It was hard to shake the feeling that everything had changed, especially with Hannah missing Caroline's presence. She missed her smile, her laugh, and the little things they used to do together.

Maggie entered her room. Hannah didn't even hear the door crack open. "I miss her, too," Maggie said, her voice low and gentle.

Hannah turned and saw her mom standing beside her, watching the video with a mellow smile. She grabbed her phone and paused the song, her finger hovering over the screen, pushing it aside.

"You know, that was one of my favorite memories. I remember telling Caroline that your father and I had a surprise for you, and she got so excited that she woke you and Sadie. You guys ate your breakfast so fast, you couldn't wait any longer," Maggie laughed.

Hannah formed a small smile and laughed half-heartedly, her stare drifting away from her mom's eyes. She felt as if she had been negative throughout the entire move and felt terrible about it. Yet, in the end, she decided not to say anything.

"Hey, Mom, do you think I'm being unrealistic?" she asked, her voice tingling with uncertainty.

"Honey, what are you talking about?" asked Maggie, looking at her with gentle eyes.

"Well …" Hannah began before letting out a deep sigh. "I mean … what if I'm not ready to make a fresh start by doing my sophomore year again at some new school? I mean … if Caroline were here … "

Maggie pulled her in for a big hug, attempting to ease her worries. "Look, I know it has been hard since she…" she said before putting on a reassuring, tender smile. "But I think starting at a new school might help you make some new friends. You know, just to get your mind off what happened. And honestly, I don't think you're being unrealistic."

 Hannah's shoulders relaxed as her mom's words wrapped around her, and a small sigh escaped her lips. "Thanks, Mom," she said, forming a small smile. Maggie kissed her on the cheek.

"Okay, I'm gonna go to the store, buy some groceries, and pick up some dinner. Sadie voted for pizza. What's your vote?" asked Maggie.

"I vote for pizza," Hannah answered quickly.
Maggie raised an eyebrow, the corner of her mouth shifting into a knowing smirk. "Let me guess: Hawaiian with extra cheese, pineapple, ham, and bacon," she said, calm but playful.

"Yep," said Hannah, revealing a more sly, playful smile.
Hannah laughed as she watched her mom leave, closing the door behind her. Then she grabbed her sketchbook, turned to the same drawing, and picked up her colored pencils. She chose a seafoam-green pencil and began coloring the fairy's intricate, well-designed dress. After an hour of

coloring, Hannah stared at the fairy's wings. She couldn't figure out what color she wanted to use. Then, she finally decided to color them sage green.

She froze as she concentrated on coloring the wings as a strange feeling washed over her. It was as if time was slipping away from her, like she was no longer in her room. Her thoughts seemed to slip away, dragged by an unseen force. Her heart pounded as her breath grew heavier. For a moment, she felt like someone or something was chasing her, stealing her thoughts from reality. Then, her mind was consumed entirely by something else—a clear vision of a fairy queen. She was tall and elegant, moving with a quiet confidence that gravitated toward her. Her dark brown, curly hair cascaded down her back in wild waves as she gracefully walked. Her dark brown eyes sparkled as she smiled. Her silver circlet crown resting on her head caught the sunlight as its emerald illuminated with an iridescent glow.

Her dress rippled around her with every graceful step as the fabric flowed effortlessly, while the asymmetrical hemline added an edge to her otherwise timeless look. The soft color of green enhanced her radiant complexion and dark hair, as if the colors complemented her perfectly. It wasn't just her dress that made her stand out. She wore a gradient pair of sage and forest-green fairy wings on her back that seemed to flutter in the fading light, creating an illusion of ethereal magic.

"Hannah?" said a voice.
Hannah gasped as she felt like she was back in the present. Her eyes blinked as the room around her returned to focus. She looked to see who had called her name—it was Sadie, standing there with a startled expression.

"Uh … Mom said pizza's here," said Sadie, her voice ambiguous.
Hannah let out a small, shaky chuckle while her hand closed her sketchbook. "Oh right, pizza," she said, her voice trailing slightly.

Sadie's brow furrowed as she tilted her head slightly. "Are you okay?" she asked.

"Yeah, uh … I must've dozed off or something," Hannah said nervously, her mind still foggy. She slowly stood up and followed Sadie down to the kitchen.

In the kitchen, Jeremy pulled the breadsticks from the microwave, letting the delicious scent fill the air. Hannah, Sadie, and Maggie ate pizza, fettuccine alfredo with chicken, and Caesar salad. Sadie poked her fork into a piece of her chicken at the table. Her brow furrowed with a hint of tension as she chewed slowly before setting her fork down with a tired sigh.

"Man, I would prefer to eat Pizza Street's alfredo instead of this," she muttered.

Hannah rolled her eyes at Sadie's comment, choosing not to say anything. "Sadie, we talked about this. I expect you to try new things instead of being picky," said Maggie, her voice stern but patient.

Sadie rolled her eyes as she poked her alfredo with her fork. "I can't wait to get to my new school to try some *real* food," she murmured.

Jeremy sat next to Sadie, holding his plate of breadsticks, a slice of pizza, his alfredo portion, and his salad.

"Oh, speaking of school," Maggie said, setting her fork down after taking a bite of her pizza. "I met this woman at the grocery store, and she said that she's a principal at the high school that Hannah is going to."

Hannah's eyes widened, her curiosity piqued. "What school?" she asked, her brow furrowed.

"Avalon High," Maggie said, her excitement carrying in her voice. "The funny thing is … I recognized her voice on the phone, and she said she approved all of Hannah's transcripts, which means Hannah is officially a student at Avalon High."

Hannah's mouth dropped open, her eyes widening as she stared at her mom. "W-wow! Uh … That's amazing," she said hesitantly.

"Wait, what school am I going to?" Sadie asked, her voice laced with curiosity and disbelief.

"You're going to Wildwood Middle School. That's where you're gonna finish your sixth grade," said Jeremy.

Sadie rolled her eyes, letting a scoff escape her lips. "This sucks. I wish we—" she said when Maggie interrupted her.

"Hey! Language!" Maggie said sternly again.

"Sorry, Mom," said Sadie, her voice flat.

Hannah's gaze drifted to her pizza, her hand secure as she lifted the slice to her mouth, blocking the voices around her. She chewed slowly, tuning out the conversation as she grabbed a napkin to wipe the sauce off the corner of her face.

After dinner, Hannah heaved a weary sigh as she glanced at her reflection in the mirror. She wore her favorite pajamas—a hunter-green V-neck, short-sleeved shirt, and matching aqua-green cotton pants. Her chocolate-brown hair, streaked with subtle copper highlights, shone in the dim light of her new bathroom. She pulled it back into a bun, securing it with her gray clip. She let out another fatigued sigh as she reached for her toothpaste and toothbrush.

She applied the paste to the bristles and began brushing her teeth. As she emerged from the bathroom, she found Sadie looking at one of her drawings.

"Don't you ever get tired of drawing these?" asked Sadie, giving her a mischievous look.

"What?" Hannah asked.
Sadie held up a drawing of a fierce battle between the fairies, with vibrant colors and intricate details. Those considered the good fairies had wings that were white or different types of bright colors, while the evil fairies had wings in darker shades, like black, red, blue, or dark purple.

"You know, someday you are gonna have to stop drawing fairies. This is not kindergarten," Sadie scoffed.

Hannah's brow scowled tightly as a vein in her temple pulsed visibly. Sadie touching her things was one of her pet peeves. It always made her skin crawl. "You know I can't do that," she said, her jaw tightening as her eyes narrowed. "I need something to take the stress out of my life. Why are you even here in my room?"

"I don't know," Sadie laughed. "I was just wondering why my sixteen-year-old sister would be *so* interested in fairies, sprites, and unicorns."

Hannah stormed toward Sadie and snatched the drawing out of her hand. "Don't you *EVER* touch my stuff again," she bellowed, her voice getting louder. "Now *GET OUT!*"

"Hey, I'm just asking why you would draw these kinds of things," Sadie whined, snatching the picture back.

Hannah's brow creased deeper, and her face flared with more irritation. She then grabbed a pillow, her fingers tightening around the summer-green fabric as if trying to hold onto something before raising it high. Sadie's eyes grew wide when she saw the pillow in Hannah's hand. With a scream, she turned and bolted for the door, letting the drawing slip through her hands as the pillow hit her back.

"Girls, go to sleep," Jeremy's tired but firm voice called from the doorway. An evil smile spread across Hannah's face as she pinned her drawing back to the wall, her hand grasping her pillow. With the noise dying down, Hannah turned off her light and climbed into bed. She grabbed her phone and tapped the alarm tab to set her alarm clock for 6:30 a.m. With her alarm set, Hannah rested her head on the softness of her pillow, closing her eyes as she drifted into a deep sleep. Suddenly, she awoke, feeling restless and struggling to fall back asleep. She tossed and turned, plagued by a recurring nightmare that had haunted her for years. At the exact moment Caroline disappeared, Hannah had just woken up from one of her nightmares—so real and intense that, for a second, she couldn't tell if she was still dreaming or not.

The nightmare always took her back to Johnson Park in Chicago, where she and Caroline had once played with their favorite yellow bouncy ball. Their laughter echoed in the air as they sang "Frère Jacques." But when Hannah threw the ball too high, it bounced away, rolling into the dark, shadowy woods. Caroline was always the brave one. She'd rush to volunteer, eager to look for the ball.

"Hannah-Banana, stay here with Sadie Tabby," she said, her voice playful yet insistent.

At the edge of the woods, Hannah stood frozen and motionless, her eyes gazing at where Caroline had disappeared. The sound of leaves crunching echoed as Caroline's footsteps faded into the distance. The woods had gone silent. Minutes had passed, and Caroline still hadn't returned. Her heart pounded loudly, and her fingers fidgeted hastily.

Panic rushed through Hannah as her feet moved forward, crunching the leaves as she walked deeper into the woods. With every step, the trees grew thicker as the breeze blew quieter. Her mind raced, and she frantically looked around the shadows, desperate to find Caroline. Suddenly, a scream shattered the silence and Hannah's thoughts. She could hear Caroline's frantic screams and cries for help resonate in the air. Her heart skipped a beat as she ran with adrenaline, but the sound of Caroline's screams seemed to move farther away.

Luckily, Hannah stumbled into a clearing—until she froze as her blood ran cold. Caroline was surrounded by twisting shadows. It reached out like long, clawed fingers, wrapping around her arms and legs, dragging her into the darkness. Breaking through the shadows' grasp, Caroline reached out her hand to Hannah, begging for her help.

 "Hannah! HELP ME! HELP ME PLEASE!" she screamed, trembling with fear.

Caroline was pulled away before Hannah could reach her, disappearing into the darkness.

"Caroline!" she screamed, stretching out her hand, but all it could hold was empty air.

Then, everything changed. She was no longer in the woods. Hannah was sixteen again, surrounded by shadows and darkness. A shadow attempted to grab her leg, and she jumped back in fear. Then, the darkness spun around her, making her dizzy as the trees and the ground vanished, replaced by a void of darkness. Her heart raced as she stared into something covered in pitch black. Yellow, glowing eyes watched her from the darkness as if they were seeing right through her. Hannah then heard unsettling voices of evil laughter echoing around her, sending shivers down her spine.

Her heart was racing as she saw shadowy hands reaching out to her. She tried to scream, but her voice was caught in her throat as if sealed shut. Fear locked her in place, her body heavy and still, as though the weight of it had turned her into lead, unable to move or even take her breath. Just as the shadows closed in, everything went black. Hannah gasped for air, her body jolting upright as she woke up. Her heart pounded in her chest, and it took a few seconds for her to realize she was safe and sound back in her bedroom. She sat up and looked around, trying to calm her racing heart. She sighed with relief.

"It's just a dream," she whispered. "Come on, Hannah. Get it together. Try to forget about her."

She glanced at her phone under her pillow. It was 2:00 a.m. Breathing heavily, she pulled her comforter and settled back into bed, trying to push away the thoughts as she drifted back to sleep. Eventually, she finally fell back into another peaceful slumber.

CHAPTER 2

The shrill beep of her phone cut through the quiet morning, startling Hannah awake. She groaned, rubbing her eyes as she reached over to silence her alarm. The clock flashed at 6:30 a.m. With a tired yawn, Hannah climbed out of bed, stretching her arms toward the ceiling, trying to shake off the drowsiness.

She turned on her portable speaker and selected one of her all-time favorite rock songs, "Rock n Roll Girl" by CC, filling the calmness with upbeat energy. The sound of electric guitars and drums filled her room, blasting through the small device, the rhythm instantly lifting her spirits. With a slight grin, Hannah stepped into her closet. She scanned through her clothes, trying to decide what to wear. After a bit of deliberation, she pulled out her top four outfits, ready to face the new day in a new school.

Her green pullover hoodie with a pocket in the middle and medium-blue skinny jeans caught her eye first, followed by a heather-gray cap-sleeve T-shirt and light blue mid-length shorts. Next, she grabbed an orange, loose-fitting scoop-neck top with navy-blue boot-cut jeans. Finally, she picked out a light blue T-shirt with a royal blue graphic star and a cerulean graphic heart, paired with dark blue skinny jeans.

Standing in front of her bed, Hannah studied each outfit before deciding on the fourth outfit, setting the others aside.

She headed to her bathroom for a quick shower and to brush her teeth. Once done, she slipped into her chosen outfit and added her blue jean jacket, perfect for balancing her casual, tomboy style with a touch of artistic flair. She picked out her favorite pair of brown boots that came halfway up her calves. Next, she moved on to her hair. After a moment of thought, she let her hair flow freely, the loose waves framing her face.

Finally, she grabbed her necklace—a golden chain with an emerald and a

Taurus sign hanging from it. She wasn't sure how long she'd had it, but it was still her favorite. Lastly, she grabbed her phone, charger, and mint-green-and-brown laptop backpack.

She headed downstairs, drawn by the strong smell of her favorite chocolate chip strawberry pancakes sizzling on the griddle—the scent of scrambled eggs intertwined with the tang of bacon and the savory freshness of avocado toast.

"Morning," she said.
"Morning, sweetie!" Maggie said, her voice full of cheerfulness.
Sadie was busy stuffing her eggs in her mouth, but she managed to speak despite having a full mouth. "Morning," she mumbled, waving her hand at Hannah.

Hannah glanced around, her eyes darting from corner to corner, landing on the empty spot at the table. "Uh, where's Dad?" she asked, her brow wrinkled while her voice was tinged with confusion.

"He just left ten minutes ago," said Maggie, not looking away from the griddle as she flipped a pancake, her focus unwavering.

Hannah released a subdued "Oh" with a drawn-out breath, her hand reaching for a plate piled with a pancake, scrambled eggs, two pieces of bacon, and one slice of avocado toast. She drizzled syrup over her pancakes and eggs and sat next to Sadie. From the living room, the TV flickered from a commercial to the news as the two sisters ate. A Hispanic man appeared on the screen, seated across from the news anchor in the background. He spoke with a serious expression and a concerned tone.

"Welcome back, everyone. Chris Gonzales here, and today, we are discussing the case of Serenity Hamilton, a fifteen-year-old student who has been missing for four months now," he said. "It is a case that has left the entire community shaken."

Looking at the news, Hannah and Sadie were frozen. Their eyes widened with shock. This was the first time they heard about it. Maggie, holding her plate with pancakes, eggs, bacon, and avocado toast, joined them at the table, completely and equally stunned.

"According to sources, Serenity Hamilton was last seen leaving home to attend a bonfire party on May 6th, just before her final exams," the news anchor continued. The scene cut to a photo of an African American teenage girl smiling confidently with black hair, beautiful brown skin, and brown eyes. "She has not been seen or heard from since then."

Hannah's heart sank even further as she stared at the image of the young girl. Then, the screen shifted, and a new face appeared—a woman with strawberry-blonde hair that seemingly caught a luminous glow in the studio, pale skin, and blue eyes. Beside her, the name "Victoria Branch" flashed briefly on the left side of the screen. The camera panned to her standing before the dense woods. The trees loomed behind her, stretching toward the sky. The ominous silence of the words hung heavily, adding to the eerie calmness.

"Yes, Chris, this is a case that has kept everyone on edge," she said, her voice loud and clear. "Her parents have been tirelessly searching for her ever since she went missing."

"Right, Victoria. Despite numerous leads and investigations, there has still been no sign of Serenity," the news anchor added. "It is a tragic situation for her family and the entire Avalon community."

Victoria nodded, her lips pressed slightly together as she processed the news. "Chris, you recently spoke to Serenity's parents, right?" she asked. "What can you tell us about their state of mind?"

The news anchor took a deep breath. "Actually, Victoria, I have not heard from her parents," he responded, the disappointment evident in his eyes. "I left a few messages, and they have not responded. I even asked them to come in for an interview, but they haven't contacted me back."

"Huh. That is strange because when a child goes missing, it's always every parent's worst nightmare," Victoria said. "It's so hard to imagine what they have been going through. Do we have any updates on the investigation?"

The news reporter shook his head slowly, letting out a heavy sigh. "Unfortunately, no. The trail seems to have gone cold, and the police are still without any solid leads," he said, his voice growing firmer despite the sadness in his eyes. "They are determined not to give up until they find Serenity."

Victoria gave a slow nod, her eyes flickering with hope as her expression softened. "Thank you, Chris. We will continue to keep our viewers updated on this case", she paused momentarily. "For AMTV News, I'm Victoria Branch."

The screen faded to black, and a commercial break came on. Hannah and Sadie sat there frozen, feeling the weight of the news sinking in. None of them said a word. They exchanged uneasy glances as if trying to piece together what might have happened to Serenity. All they could do was sit silently, their minds racing, struggling to understand. As the TV switched back to the news, Maggie quickly grabbed the remote and pressed the power button, turning it off with a sharp click.

"Come on, guys, I can't be late for work, and you cannot be late for your first day," she said, shaky despite maintaining her cheerfulness. "Let's go."

The girls hurriedly grabbed their backpacks, ready to head out the door. Hannah barely noticed, completely lost in her music as "Rush" by Aly & AJ blasted through her AirPods. They stood by, watching as their mom unlocked the door to her green Lexus NX.

"Hurry up, girls," Maggie called out to them.

"Geez, Mom, we're coming," Sadie groaned, rolling her eyes.
The girls climbed into the car, but Hannah was still lost in her music, her mind drifting far from her surroundings. She didn't notice the world outside as they drove toward the school. Her gaze drifted out the window, watching the houses and trees blur past as her mind wandered elsewhere. She wasn't just thinking about her first day at her new school. She was also thinking about Caroline's and Serenity's disappearances as they weighed heavily on her thoughts. As they neared a particular intersection, Maggie slowed the car.

 Hannah snapped out of her trance, realizing they had finally reached Avalon High. Her stomach churned as she stared at the unfamiliar school building. She wished she were back in the familiar halls of North Liberty High in Chicago, surrounded by her old friends and teachers.

"I don't know if I can do this," she said, her voice tinged with uncertainty. Maggie's hand rested lightly on her shoulder, the warmth of her touch melting some of the tension in her body.

"Hey, remember what I said when you started your first day of kindergarten?" she asked, a smile tugging at the corners of her lips.

Hannah paused for a moment, trying to remember her mom's words, before nodding slowly. "Don't let the nerves take control of you. Think of happiness and excitement, and let that help you through your day," she said.

Hannah smiled. "Except I'm not five anymore," she said, her voice gentle and soothing.

"Hannah—" said Maggie sternly, her brow creasing.
Hannah let out a heavy sigh, a brief smile curving across the corner of her lips. "Alright, thanks, Mom," she said.

Maggie hugged her tightly, kissing her forehead as her tone softened. "I love you, Hannah-Banana," she said, her voice becoming more cheerful again.

"I love you, too," said Hannah, her tone subdued though a little distant. Hannah grabbed her backpack and stepped out of the car. She turned to her mom and smiled. She waved while Sadie stuck her tongue out as the car pulled away. She removed her AirPods, catching a brief moment to take in the sight before her.

The school grounds were expansive, with perfectly manicured lawns and vibrant flower gardens lining the winding pathways. The sun poured down on the maroon brick building, casting a warm glow over the entire area. The three-story main building stood tall in the center of the campus, a modern architectural masterpiece. Two rows of beautiful white columns lined the archway, adding a touch of elegance and sophistication to the otherwise modern building.

Directly underneath the archway was the main entrance to the school. The front entrance was grand, with large double doors flanked by two towering pillars. Two large glass doors, surrounded by sleek metal framing, provided a glimpse into the bustling hallways that lay beyond. Above the door, the school's name, "Avalon High School," was engraved in bold letters, proudly showing its identity.

The bustling courtyard was in front of the building, where the students scattered about. Some sat on the benches, chatting lively, while others headed toward their classes. The school's spirit flag, with its bold panther mascot, fluttered proudly in the light breeze, encouraging a strong sense of pride and community. Shades of colors embellished the wall, with vibrant posters and banners celebrating the school's various sports teams and extracurricular activities.

As she walked toward the school's entrance, she could hear conversations and laughter from the students already gathered inside. She let out a lingering breath as she kept walking, her thoughts swirling around her. Lost in her thoughts, Hannah didn't notice a woman heading in the opposite direction until they bumped into each other with a light thud.

She stumbled back, her face almost flushing with embarrassment. "Oh, I'm sorry. I didn't see you there," she apologized quickly.

The Chinese American woman had black, curly hair pulled back into a neat ponytail. Her brown eyes sparkled with excitement, and she had fair skin that contrasted beautifully with her crisp white chiffon blouse, classic collar, black business pants, and black ballet flats, professional yet approachable.

"It's no problem," the woman replied, her lips curving into a warm, friendly smile. "Are you a new student here?"

Hannah nodded, relieved that the woman didn't seem upset by her clumsiness.

"Fantastic!" the woman exclaimed. "My name is Mrs. Liu, and I'm the vice principal. It is so great to have you here."

Hannah shifted uncomfortably, pulling the strap of her backpack as she looked into Mrs. Liu's kind eyes. The thought of being the new student in a strange school made her feel out of place. But Mrs. Liu's heartfelt smile and welcome eased some of her nerves.

"I'm Hannah. Hannah Sumpter," she said, offering a friendly but shy smile.

"Well, it's nice to meet you, Hannah," Mrs. Liu replied. "I was planning on returning to Ms. Caldwell's office, but I can let her know that you're here, and we'll get you settled in for your first day."

"Cool," said Hannah, her smile becoming more reassuring and confident. Hannah followed Mrs. Liu down the brightly decorated hallways of the school, their footsteps echoing indistinctly against the polished, tiled floors. The walls were painted in their school colors of royal purple, white, and black, lined with posters and banners displaying the achievements of the students. As they walked, Hannah couldn't help but notice how nice the school was, with all its features. Students were rushing to their classes, others were sitting in the courtyard chatting, and some gathered in the cafeteria. She thought this school reminded her somewhat of North Liberty, if not better. It was difficult not to feel optimistic about what her first day might hold because the hallways were equally bright, and the environment was new and exciting.

"Wow! This school is quite something," Hannah remarked, taken in by the bustling atmosphere.

Mrs. Liu's lips curved into a proud smile, her eyes sparkling as she spoke. "Yes, we take pride in our students and their achievements," she said. "We also strongly focus on diversity and creating a welcoming environment for all students." Hannah could sense the strict yet genuine care behind her words, and shortly enough, the weight of her nervousness faded away.

 Mrs. Liu stopped in front of Hannah, her posture still standing tall. "Tell you what, you wait here while I go inform Ms. Caldwell"? she said, her tone reassuring. "That way, we can set up your classes and schedule at once."

As Mrs. Liu walked away, Hannah found herself lost in her thoughts. She glanced around the hallway, admiring the style. Small conversations and lockers slamming filled the air, making the school feel almost alive. Hannah's eyes grew enlarged as her gaze shifted from one sight to the next.

Lost in her thoughts, Hannah rounded a corner and barely noticed a girl stepping out of a classroom until they collided. The girl let out a sharp gasp as her books scattered across the floor. Hannah quickly stepped back, her eyes gaping in shock.

"Watch where you're going!" the girl snapped, her voice laced with annoyance.

"Sorry," Hannah quickly apologized, bending down to help pick up the books.

As she gathered them, Hannah couldn't help but briefly glance at the girl's appearance—platinum blonde hair, fair skin, and piercing green eyes. She wore a pink mesh long-sleeved shirt, a black high-waisted flared skirt, and chunky high-heeled shoes—the perfect epitome of a typical mean girl. Hannah stood up and handed the books back to her. Three other girls had already joined her before Hannah could say another word.

They exchanged smug glances, and Hannah's stomach churned, sending a wave of discomfort washing over her. One girl with brown hair, fair skin, and brown eyes even gave Hannah's outfit a dismissive look, letting out a scoff.

"Are you from Wisconsin or something?" she asked, dripping with condescension.

Hannah was about to correct her when she noticed two other girls—one with brown skin, black hair, and warm brown eyes—were snickering behind the platinum-blonde and brown-haired girl. She had never dealt with mean girls before, until now. "No, I'm from Chicago," she said.

The light, natural blonde-haired girl with green eyes and fair skin leaned in on the platinum-blonde, apparently the clique's leader. "Hey Heather, aren't girls from Chicago supposed to be chic?" she asked, her voice rising with sarcasm.

The girl named *Heather* made a fake shocked gasp and turned to Hannah, her lips curving into a smug smirk. "Oh yeah, Chicago girls are supposed to be pretty, prim, and chic," she said disdainfully. "I never thought they would let outsiders like you transfer here."

Hannah's brow crinkled in confusion, and her fists slightly clenched as her heart sank at Heather's cruel words. She felt like tears were about to come out of her eyes, but she refused to let someone like Heather intimidate her. She squared her shoulders and spoke firmly. "Actually, my *name* is Hannah."

Heather burst into laughter, and the other girls joined in, their giggles mocking. They turned and walked away before Hannah could respond, leaving her alone in the hallway. Her cheeks flushed in embarrassment, and her heart ached, but she held her ground. Despite the hurtful words sinking into her mind, Hannah brushed it off as she prepared to continue her first day.

"Hannah?" said a voice ringing in her ears.
A startled Hannah turned around, wondering who had called her name. It was Mrs. Liu standing in front of her. Her pleasant smile instantly eased her tense and awkward encounter with Heather and her friends.

"Sorry, uh … Ms. Caldwell is here to see you," she said.
Hannah trailed behind Mrs. Liu down the hallway, her heart pounding so loudly it refused to stop. With every step toward the principal's office, she could feel her palms sweating and a knot forming in her stomach. She had never been to the principal's office before. The thought of meeting her new principal on her first day made her even more nervous. Hannah exhaled forcefully as Mrs. Liu opened the door, releasing her nerves.

The principal, a woman with warm medium-copper hair, green eyes, and fair skin, awaited them. She wore a professional outfit: an orange blouse with long sleeves under a black blazer paired with dark gray pants and slate-colored high heels. The principal's eyebrows clenched as she looked at Hannah, her eyes narrowing in recognition. She froze, unable to come up with the words. For a moment, she seemed lost in thought. Before she could speak, Mrs. Liu cleared her throat loudly, snapping her out of her trance.

"Ms. Caldwell, this is Hannah Sumpter," Mrs. Liu said, introducing her warmly. "She's the new student we were expecting today."

Ms. Caldwell's friendly smile grew as she extended her hand. "Welcome to our school, Hannah," she beamed.

Hannah shook her hand, her shaky fingers loosening their tight grip. The principal seemed friendlier than her old principal back in North Liberty. As Ms. Caldwell smiled, Hannah noticed her green eyes seemingly distant, as if they didn't quite match the warmth of her expression. For a moment, Hannah wondered if there was more to Ms. Caldwell than she let on. Ms. Caldwell turned to Mrs. Liu with a smile. Her mysterious eyes changed, replaced by a geniality that reached her lips.

"Thank you for bringing her in, Mrs. Liu," she said in a calm, kind voice. "You may go now."

Mrs. Liu nodded and left the room, leaving Hannah alone with Ms. Caldwell. Hannah followed her across the room toward a girl sitting in the corner. The girl had a tan complexion, curly, dark brown hair framing her face, and dark brown eyes that sparkled when she looked at Hannah and Ms. Caldwell. She wore a green V-neck plaid blouse, black leggings, and black high-top sneakers. Hannah could tell that they were around the same age. The girl stood at an impressive height of 5'9" and had a tomboyish style similar to Hannah's but with a sporty, chic twist that gave it a sharp edge.

"Before we go over your schedule, I would like to introduce you to Sydney Barnes," Ms. Caldwell said. "She will help you navigate your classes and get acquainted with the school."

Sydney flashed a warm smile at Hannah and extended her hand. "Hi, it's nice to meet you," she said, her voice friendly and genuine.

Hannah shook her hand, returning the smile to Sydney. Sydney's friendly demeanor was a huge breath of fresh air after her rocky encounter with Heather and her friends. "Nice to meet you, too," she said.

Ms. Caldwell motioned for both girls to sit in front of her desk before stepping out to the printing center. Sydney leaned in toward Hannah. "We have geometry, English, and culinary arts together," she said, her voice barely above a whisper. "Oh, and we also have homeroom together."

As Hannah nodded at the information, Ms. Caldwell returned, handing her a paper with her class schedule and an agenda. Hannah studied her schedule, feeling grateful for Sydney's kindness.

"Your new counselor has already selected your classes for the semester," Ms. Caldwell explained. "Your student ID is next to your locker number, which is 110, along with your combination. You will be in Farrow's homeroom, Reza's English II class, Fontaine's French II class, Chavez's Geometry class, Lombardi's Culinary Arts I class, Knowles's Drawing & Painting II class, and Snyder's U.S. History class. You'll also have Hamilton for Chemistry I."

Hannah took a deep breath, impressed by the variety of classes she would attend. A mixture of excitement and nerves about starting in a new school rushed inside her.

"Thanks for your help," she said before standing up.
Hannah and Sydney left the office together, walking side by side through the wide hallways on their way to their first-period class.

"So, this is the main building," Sydney said, pointing to a large red building with white columns at the entrance. "Most of your classes will be here, except for the gym and the science labs, which are in the white building over there, away from the entrance."

Hannah nodded, her eyes scanning the bustling hallways as each noise and movement overwhelmed her senses. More students crowded the lockers while some hurried to their next class. Laughter and conversations reverberated in the halls. Sydney continued the tour, leading Hannah through the school's key spots—from the library to the cafeteria and, finally, the auditorium.

As they made their way to Reza's class, Sydney warned Hannah about their third-period class with Chavez. "Oh, and be prepared for Mr. Chavez's class," she said. "He's super strict about everything. You do not want to get on his bad side," she added, her expression serious but playful.

Hannah nodded, bracing herself for the class ahead. She needed to be on her best behavior and avoid trouble with Mr. Chavez.

"Don't worry, Ms. Reza is the complete opposite," Sydney continued as they turned a corner. "She's really nice and super lenient with deadlines if you talk to her beforehand. She's always so helpful and understanding. Honestly, she's a real gem of a teacher. She's so passionate about her job and is really sweet, intelligent, and a genuine soul."

Hannah nodded, listening to Sydney's words. As they walked through the hallways, the two girls chatted easily, exchanging questions and stories to learn more about each other. Hannah felt a wave of happiness, thrilled to find a friend so quickly, especially since she was the new girl in school.

"So, are you a sophomore?" Sydney asked, raising her eyebrow in curiosity.

Hannah nodded, relieved that they were in the same grade. "Yeah, I am," she replied.

"That's awesome! I'm a sophomore too," Sydney exclaimed, her voice filled with clear excitement.

Hannah smiled and nodded again, feeling more at ease with each passing moment. She was starting to warm up to Sydney as they enjoyed their conversation. As they walked down the hallway, the two girls continued to ask each other more questions, still learning a little more about each other.

"So, where did you move from?" Sydney asked, her voice still curious. "My family and I moved from Chicago," Hannah explained. "My mom just accepted a new accounting job. She was this close to transferring me to East Avalon High."

"That's cool. At least you didn't go there because the coaches are so hardcore," Sydney laughed. "Speaking of coaches, do you play any sports?"

Hannah shook her head, a shy smile forming on her lips. "Actually, I'm more of an artsy, creative type, but I do play some sports," she said, subtly angling her head.

Sydney nodded with enthusiasm. "I play center forward on the junior varsity soccer team. I'm also the co-captain. You should come to one of our games sometime," she said, her enthusiasm brightening her words.

Hannah smiled warmly, her excitement matching Sydney's. "I'll definitely try to make it," she said.

Sydney's eyes brightened when she noticed Hannah's necklace. "Hey, I've got one like that!" she exclaimed. "Mine's November 29th. What about yours?"

Hannah's eyes blinked, stopping her in her tracks while her mouth hung open. "No way," she said, her smile warm and genuine. "I was born on May 15th."

Sydney smiled and pulled out her necklace, holding it out for Hannah to see. It was identical to Hannah's, except hers had an orange topaz and a golden Sagittarius sign hanging from it. "Looks like we have a lot more in common than we thought," she joked.

The two girls laughed as they exchanged phone numbers, Instagram handles, and Snapchat usernames, excited to stay in touch. Their conversation continued as they made their way into Ms. Reza's class.

CHAPTER 3

The teacher seemed to be Persian, with fair skin that seemed to glow under the classroom light. She had long, dark brown hair and brown eyes that sparkled whenever she spoke. She wore a lengthy, flowing black dress with pleats and a V-neck wrap paired with black pointed-toe ballet flats, giving her a sophisticated, elegant look.

She stopped mid-sentence as soon as she noticed Sydney and Hannah walking in. Even though they were late, the teacher's warm smile never disappeared, still curving across her face as she greeted them. "Hello, Sydney, so nice of you to join us," she said, her voice crisp and clear.

"Sorry, Ms. Reza," Sydney apologized before finding a seat in the back row.

Ms. Reza then turned to Hannah next, her smile growing friendlier. "Hi, you must be the new student here," she said. "Welcome to our class."

Hannah nervously nodded, her fingers twisting the edges as she handed her schedule to Ms. Reza. She glanced over it, eyes scanning before briefly meeting Ms. Reza's look of understanding. Then she glanced back at the schedule. "English II with Ms. Reza. You are in the right class," she said, reassuring and warm.

Ms. Reza handed Hannah *The Great Gatsby* book and explained that the class was currently working on identifying vocabulary words from the book. She also gave her a syllabus, reminding her to get her parents' signature and to return it by Monday.

As the lesson began, Hannah couldn't help but admire Ms. Reza's teaching style. Her passion for literature was contagious, and she had a unique way of explaining things that made the class even more interesting and engaging. Hannah remembered how Sydney had spoken so highly of her, and now, sitting in her class, she could see why. Ms. Reza was different from her old English teacher back in North Liberty. The more Hannah listened, the more she discovered she admired Ms. Reza and her eloquent and fluent teachings, which made the English class feel alive and exciting.

As the last bell rang, signaling the end of their third-period class, Sydney and Hannah packed their backpacks and headed into the crowded hallway.

"I can't believe Mr. Chavez gave me homework," Hannah scowled, her voice filled with frustration. I mean, how does a teacher give homework on the first day of school?"

Sydney let out a small laugh, rolling her eyes. "I tried to warn you. He's notorious for that," she said.

Hannah let out a loud groan, dropping her head slightly. Then suddenly, Sydney stopped and turned to Hannah with a mischievous grin. "Hey, have you heard about Panther Time?" she asked.

Hannah knitted her eyebrows, her curiosity intrigued. "Panther Time? What's that?" she asked, her eyes lifting with interest.

"It happens on Thursdays and Fridays," Sydney explained. "Since today is Thursday, we can get extra help, work on homework, attend tutoring, join study sessions, or even attend workshops. We can also hang out with friends and classmates."

Hannah's eyes snapped open, her interest piqued. "That's so cool! I've never had that before," she said, her voice brimming with excitement.

Sydney swept a strand of her hair behind her ear. "You know, I'm heading to the cafeteria to grab a snack. You wanna come?" she asked.

Hannah smiled. "Count me in," she said eagerly.
The two girls headed toward the cafeteria, passing students to different locations, from study halls to computer labs, clubs, and other activities.

When they reached the cafeteria, Hannah couldn't help but admire the unique design. It was nothing like what she was used to at her old school. The area was more modern, giving it a lively, welcoming vibe.

The area appeared expansive, with towering glass walls, allowing sunlight to flood in, giving the space a fragile yet celestial quality. It resembled an insight into the future. The elevated ceiling skylights grandly above, garnished with refined metal beams, provided natural light into the room. Hannah wandered in awe, taking in the polished concrete walls, creating a unique and vigorous atmosphere. The scene was accented solely by the lively stained glass panel that radiated with vivid colors and liveliness. The smooth marble floors gleamed under her feet, and she felt like they were floating with each step she took.

At the center of the cafeteria was an interactive screen, constantly flashing artwork and stories from students, upcoming events, and even live feeds of the school's sports games. The screen seemed to pulse with the rhythm of the life of the school, drawing every student's and teacher's attention.

At the back of the cafeteria, cozy booths lined the walls with modern, high-top tables that filled the space. The food stations featured an array of choices: A fresh salad bar sparkled under golden lights, and the sandwich station provided a variety of hearty, flavorful options. The hot food counter was particularly inviting, thanks to the savory scent and the sizzling sound of the food as students moved through the line.

Nearby the salad bar, the smoothie bar unleashed the fruity aroma of different fruits and citrus, while the juice counter offered a cool and refreshing taste. The dessert counter was a delightful temptation, with vibrant desserts, from cookies to baklava to cupcakes. A snack bar, ice cream counter, and a milkshake machine allowed the creation of personal favorites to indulge any craving and offer a perfect individual delight.

"Whoa, this is amazing," Hannah murmured, her eyes darting across the space.

Sydney grinned, noticing Hannah's wandering eyes. "Pretty cool, huh? They just added the new milkshake machine this year," she said.

As they walked toward the milkshake machine, Sydney explained to Hannah how it worked. "If there's a flavor you like, just pick it, and the machine will make it for you," she said, a grin spreading across her face.

Hannah watched Sydney tap the Kit-Kat button on the screen, and the machine came to life, blending the flavors with precision. Hannah's eyes grew wide in amazement as the machine neatly created Sydney's milkshake, letting the rich smell of chocolate fill the air. Once her milkshake was completely blended, Sydney pulled it out of the machine, took a sip, and smiled brightly. "See? It's easy. Now you try," she said.

Hannah's eyes lit up as she scanned through the options. Her gaze finally landed on Oreo. Like Sydney's, the machine hummed to life again, blending the ingredients perfectly. Hannah's mesmerized eyes watched as the machine swirled around the flavors effortlessly. With her milkshake fully blended, she gripped the handle and pulled it out of the machine.

"Wow, that's awesome," she said, her excitement almost palpable. Sydney's lips formed into a smile as she pulled out her phone, her fingers lingering above the screen. "Oh, that reminds me, I have a meeting with the literary magazine club," she said.

Hannah's eyes grew wide, her eyebrow puckering in curiosity. "Wait, so, not only are you part of the soccer team, but you're also in the literary magazine club?" she asked, tilting her head.

"Yeah," Sydney said. "I'm in charge of maintaining the magazine's social media."

"Well, my old school didn't have a literary magazine club. They only had a yearbook club," Hannah replied, sweeping a strand of hair behind her ear.

Sydney laughed at Hannah's joke. "Well, it's a good thing you came here," she said, still laughing as she walked away.

After Sydney left, Hannah took a long sip of her milkshake, a smile pulling at her lips as she looked at her schedule. Suddenly, someone crashed into her from behind, rocking her forward. Her milkshake slipped through her hand, splattering across her shirt and the left sleeve of her jacket. Her shocked gasp drew the attention of the other students, all eyes turning toward her. When she glanced up, she saw Heather and her friends standing behind her, snickering. It was clear that they crashed into her on purpose.

As Hannah stood there, milkshake dripping down her jacket sleeve, she realized she wasn't alone. A girl, appearing to be Korean American, stood nearby, equally shocked. She had auburn-red hair cascading around her shoulders; her fair skin was lightly streaked with milkshake. Her striking green-hazel eyes widened with shock, and she stood about 5'8", making her a bit taller than Hannah. Her black crew-neck T-shirt with white stripes was now splattered with milkshake. The mess had spread to her light blue cuff skinny jeans and white low-top sneakers. The girl's vibe was similar to Hannah's and Sydney's—tomboyish but with a more urban and edgy feel. She furiously waved her arm, trying to shake the stain off her sleeve, but the milkshake clung to the fabric stubbornly.

Heather's smirk deepened as she and her friends stared at Hannah and the girl. "Oops, sorry," she said, her voice dripping with a fake kindness, clearly not apologetic. "I guess I didn't see you there."

The Korean American girl's face twisted in rage as her eyes locked onto Heather's. "Are you serious?!" she screamed, her voice cracking with fury. Without another word, the girl charged toward Heather, intending to push her, but in the process, she accidentally knocked Hannah off balance. Hannah stumbled and fell to the ground with a thud.

"Ms. Park, stop!" Mrs. Liu yelled, rushing toward her, her voice firm as she pushed the girl back, trying to calm her down.

"She just knocked her shake all over me!" the girl yelled, pointing at Heather.

Heather's expression shifted instantly. Her smirk melted away as she adopted a feigned calm demeanor. "I would never do such a thing," she said, sweeping her hair back and her eyes narrowing dismissively.

"Whatever she's saying, she is lying," the girl yelled, still fuming with rage. "She started it!"

Mrs. Liu, with her voice firm yet calm, urged both girls to leave and clean themselves up. The Korean American girl grabbed her sleek, black sling convertible backpack and black hoodie in a swift grasp. Without a word, she stormed out of the cafeteria before screaming, "I hate this place!" at the top of her lungs for everyone to hear. Her heavy footsteps echoed in the hallway. Hannah's eyes softened with sympathy, a twinge of sadness stirring within her as she watched the girl, feeling a flicker of sorrow. Heather resumed her evil smirk as she waved, strutting away with her friends.

"Oh my gosh, Hannah! Are you okay?" Sydney asked, rushing over to help her up.

"Yeah, I'm okay," Hannah said. "Who is that girl?"
"That's Heather Barringer. She's one of the meanest girls in school, along with Carleigh Schmidt, Molly Vaughn, and Kaliyah Durran. You do not wanna cross them," Sydney said, her voice low before her eyes turned to Hannah. "Anyway, I have a hoodie that you can borrow. I'll see if I can remove the stain on your jacket and shirt."

Hannah nodded, her lips curving into a thin smile as she and Sydney picked up the mess, their moves gentle and steady. Even though she was still in shock, Sydney's humility eased the tension in the air. She couldn't help but feel grateful for her kindness. As her eyes drifted to Heather and her friends, sitting at a table and having a conversation, a wave of confusion swept over her, questions swirling in her head.

After fourth period, Hannah rushed to meet Sydney in the cafeteria. She hurried through the busy hallways, wearing Sydney's royal purple hoodie with the Panthers' logo on the front. It was a little oversized on her, but it was better than wearing her stained shirt and jacket.

Finally, the lunch bell rang, cutting through the voices in the hallways. Hannah spotted Sydney at the table near the exit door, eating General Tso's chicken. Their eyes widened with elation as Hannah made her way over there, sitting down across from Sydney.

"Hey," she said softly. "Thanks again for letting me borrow your hoodie." Sydney's eyes brightened with understanding, giving a tiny nod, her expression warm. "No problem," she said.

Hannah let out a small chuckle, her shoulders relaxing. "So, did you manage to get that milkshake stain out of my shirt and jacket?" she asked, a playful glint in her eyes.

Sydney nodded subtly, her lips curving into a kind smile. "Yep, easy-peasy," she said. "I used some soap and water from the bathroom. I had to put them in a plastic bag to keep them from getting everything wet in my backpack."

Sydney pulled out a small white plastic bag from her gray laptop backpack, which had a simple style, and handed it to Hannah. Hannah opened the bag and pulled out her shirt and jacket, both miraculously spotless. "Wow, you're like a stain-removing ninja," she exclaimed, clearly impressed.

Sydney laughed, her eyes sparkling. "Well, I happen to know a lot of tricks," she said, grinning. "Thanks to my sister, Kennedy."

Hannah flashed Sydney another grin, but her smile quickly faded as she shifted from side to side and leaned forward, her curiosity growing. "So these girls—Heather Barringer, Carleigh Schmidt, Kaliyah Durran, and Molly Vaughn—what's the deal with them?" she asked, crinkling her brow.

Sydney shrugged, her expression turning serious. "I don't know. They think they run the school with an iron fist or something," she explained. "Heather is the worst of them all. She's always bossing people around, making snide comments, and trying to make people believe her over others. Just yesterday, they made fun of some girl and called her a loser because of how she dressed."

"Hi," a voice called behind them, making Hannah and Sydney spin around. They both froze, eyes popping open when they unexpectedly saw a familiar face—the Korean American girl who knocked Hannah over earlier and nearly tried to start a fight with Heather. She stood there, wearing the same black hoodie, likely trying to cover the stain on her shirt.

"I'm really sorry about earlier," the girl said, looking genuinely apologetic. "I didn't know it was your milkshake. I thought it was Heather's."

Hannah and Sydney exchanged a surprised glance, taken aback by the girl's sudden change in attitude. The fiery spark in her eyes was gone, replaced by an uncertain expression. Her gaze briefly darted to the floor, then back up to meet theirs. Her eyebrows drew together with genuine regret as if she were struggling to find the right words.

The girl continued before either of them could even respond, her voice barely above a whisper. "I also wanted to ask if I could sit with you guys," she mumbled. "I...don't have anyone to sit with."

Hannah and Sydney exchanged glances, their eyes widening for a second, caught off guard by the girl's request. Hannah shifted uncomfortably in her seat, her fork tapping on the edge of her tray. She and Sydney looked at the girl, then at the two milkshakes she held in her hands—one with M&M's and the other with Oreos.

Sensing their hesitation, the girl spoke up again, breaking the silence and tension. "I promise I'm not here to cause any trouble. I even bought a milkshake for myself and another Oreo shake for you," she said, holding the Oreo shake out for Hannah to see. "I thought you might need this…since…Heather messed up your outfit."

Hannah hesitated for a moment, her eyes staring at the Oreo milkshake before reaching for it, her movements slow and unsure. "Uh … thanks," she said, her voice low and uncertain. Sydney bit her lip, then moved her backpack beside her, clearing a spot for her before a gentle smile tugged at her lips.

"You're … welcome to sit with us," she said. "I'm Sydney, by the way." Hannah gave a light nod, a friendly smile forming across her lips. "I'm Hannah. I just transferred here," she said, her voice becoming warmer as the uncertainty in her eyes faded.

Despite their greetings, Hannah and Sydney exchanged hesitant glances. Sydney slowly took a bite of her salad while Hannah absently swirled her straw around, leaving the blended whipped cream sink into the mixture.

The girl smiled meekly, her shoulders relaxing a little. "Zoey," she said, her voice ringing in a shy yet polite tone. "I'm … also in Ms. Reza's and Mr. Chavez's class with you guys."

Hannah and Sydney nodded, feeling a bit more at ease with Zoey now that they knew her name. The conversation picked up again, and Hannah couldn't help but bring up the topic again. "I never understood why some people feel the need to put others down to make themselves feel better," she said, shaking her head.

Hearing Hannah's words ringing in her ears, Zoey jumped into the conversation, her voice dripping with sarcasm. "Oh yeah, let's not forget to mention that she's daddy's little girl who thinks she's the queen of her castle and can control this whole school," she said, rolling her eyes as she mimicked Heather's smug attitude.

Hannah and Sydney snickered at Zoey's sarcastic remark, lightening up the mood as the tension in the air lifted away. Despite being a little guarded and unsure, they felt themselves starting to warm up to her, and their shoulders relaxed.

"Sorry, I didn't mean to say that," Zoey apologized.
"It's okay," said Hannah, her voice reassuring. "You're right. It's a good thing I don't deal with mean girls."

Zoey's lips shifted into a grin, a sense of relief washing over her as she realized she'd made a good impression. She glanced up from her milkshake, her gaze drifting toward Hannah's and Sydney's necklaces. Her eyebrow crinkled as she leaned in just a little.

"You know, I have that same necklace!" she exclaimed, her eyes lighting up as she pointed at it. "But mine has an amethyst and my zodiac sign, Aquarius. I was born on February 5th."

Hannah and Sydney exchanged stunned looks, their eyebrows raised in sync. They leaned in to get a better look at Zoey's necklace, and sure enough, it was identical to theirs, except with an amethyst and a golden Aquarius sign hanging from it.

"I've had this necklace since I was born, and I never take it off," Zoey continued as her fingers gently brushed the charms.

"Same," said Hannah.

"Ditto," Sydney added with a grin.

"So what's your sign?" Zoey inquired, her head angled a bit.

Hannah smiled while lifting her necklace, the charms catching the light. "I'm a Taurus. I was born on May 15th," she said.

Sydney pulled out her necklace, grinning. "I'm a Sagittarius," she said, her voice proud but warm. "I was born on November 29th."

The girls shared a laugh, their moment feeling lighter, their bond growing stronger every second. Hannah knew that her mom had been right all along. Making new friends was a great way to take her mind off Caroline.

Just then, someone called Sydney's name. Sydney turned around to see a girl standing behind her, her dirty blonde hair in a messy bun, leaving strands framing her face. The girl had pale skin and striking green eyes that seemingly sparkled. She stood about 5'9" tall, the same height as Sydney. She wore a casual red sweatshirt, black leggings, and black low-top sneakers.

Another girl, Hispanic, appeared beside her, catching the attention of the three girls. She had olive skin and dark brown curly hair with subtle caramel highlights glimmering in the light. Standing about 5'7" tall, the same height as Hannah, she had hazel eyes that seemed to shine with a lively energy. She was dressed more femininely in her rose-red lace V-neck top with puffed long sleeves, dark blue bootcut jeans, and taupe ballet flats. Compared to the trio's tomboyish style, this girl's look was trendy, sophisticated, and girly.

"Can I borrow your history notes?" the girl with dirty blonde hair asked, her voice a little timid.

Sydney's eyes lit up, and a broad smile appeared as she quickly recognized her. "Sure, no problem, Rach," she replied.

Sydney turned to Hannah and Zoey. "Oh, I almost forgot," she explained.

"Hannah, Zoey, this is Rachelle Underwood. She and I have been best friends since the fifth grade."

"Hi," Hannah said, her lips curving into a bashful but friendly smile.

"What's up?" said Zoey.

Rachelle gave a quick wave to Hannah and Zoey and then turned back to Sydney while she handed her orange notebook to her. Her eyes darted nervously as she bit her lip.

"So … Sydney," she began, her quiet voice rising with wariness. "I need your advice. There's this guy in my history class that I really like, but I have no idea how to talk to him. What should I do?"

Sydney leaned in, her gaze focused and encouraging as she met Rachelle's. Hannah and Zoey moved a little closer, exchanging curious glances. "I think you should just be yourself and talk to him," she said. "Guys like a girl who's confident and authentic."

Rachelle nodded happily, a gleeful smile widening as her eyes perked up. "Cool, thanks, Syd. See you in PE class!" she said before turning and walking down the hall.

Just before she walked off with Rachelle, the Hispanic girl, who had been quietly observing, stepped closer to Hannah. She slowly tilted her head, eyes fixed on her necklace. "Cool necklace," she said.

"Thanks," Hannah said, watching as the Hispanic girl turned and walked away.

Hannah turned back to Sydney and Zoey with a thin smile. "Like I said, if Heather and the other girls are trying to get under your skin, I've got your guys' back," said a reassuring Sydney.

Hannah and Zoey smiled, feeling that they had each other's backs, unleashing the strength of their friendship. "I almost forgot. Do you wanna exchange phone numbers?" asked Sydney.

Zoey smiled, her eyes peaking with interest. "Definitely," she said, her voice now filled with cheerfulness.

"Hey, let's make a group chat," said Hannah.
Sydney and Zoey nodded in agreement. They quickly exchanged phone numbers, Instagram handles, and Snapchat usernames. They even set up group chats from each app, from iMessage to Snapchat, ensuring they'd stay connected.

The final bell rang, and the hallways swarmed with the usual rush of students. Hannah, now wearing her thoroughly dried shirt and jacket, Sydney, and Zoey gathered their backpacks and made their way through the bustling crowd. Hannah felt her phone vibrate in her pocket as they neared the main entrance. She pulled it out, reading a text from her mom:

"Will be late. Had to pick up Sadie from school. Your father just got home. There's leftover pizza, alfredo, and salad in the fridge," the text message read.

Hannah sighed faintly, slipping her phone into her jacket pocket. "What's wrong?" Zoey asked, her eyes softening, watching Hannah adjust the strap of her backpack.

"My mom's running late," Hannah replied, holding her phone to show Sydney and Zoey. "She had to pick up my little sister, Sadie."

Zoey's brow puckered with sympathy, giving Hannah a gentle pat on the back. "That sucks. I'm sorry," she said.

Sydney, who was listening to their conversation, smiled and spoke up. "Well, I can give you a ride home if you want," she responded, gesturing to the parking lot. "My car's parked outside."

Hannah's face lit up, and relief washed over her. "Really? That would be amazing," she said. "Thank you so much."

Sydney smiled and turned to Zoey, her eyes brightening. "I can give you a ride, too, if you want," she said, her tone inviting.

Zoey hesitated, thinking for a moment before shaking her hand. "No, it's okay," she said. "My mom's picking me up. Thanks anyway."

The two girls said goodbye to Zoey and approached the parking lot. Sydney pulled out her keys, clicking the button to unlock her car. They walked to a sleek white Nissan Sentra, its exterior illuminating in the afternoon sunlight. Hannah hopped into the passenger seat, admiring the black interior's glossiness and smoothness as she buckled up. Sydney made her way to the driver's side, leaving Hannah to take a moment to look around. The car had a clean, modern feel, with black seats and a polished, refined dashboard. Her eyes landed on an orange wooden beaded ball tassel hanging from the rearview mirror, adding a pop of color to the interior.

"Whoa, this is a nice car," she said, her voice full of awe.
"Thanks! It was a birthday present from my parents last year," Sydney replied, her hands landing on the steering wheel as she started the engine. The car hummed to life as Sydney smoothly pulled out of the parking lot.

The cool breeze flowed through the windows as they drove through the streets. They chatted and laughed, their voices combining with the hum of the car. Hannah felt a sense of happiness rushing inside her, replacing the grief she'd been keeping inside her. She had made not one but two new friends. Before long, the car slowly halted as they reached the front of Hannah's house. She unbuckled her seatbelt, pushed the door open, and stepped out of the car.

"Thanks for the ride," she said, a smile tugging at her lips.

"Anytime. See you tomorrow," Sydney said, waving goodbye.

Hannah waved goodbye, watching Sydney's car disappear down the street, leaving the sound of the engine fading into the distance. With a sense of satisfaction, she turned and headed inside, hit by the sound of the indistinct conversations reverberating through the house. She spotted her dad in the living room, his eyes glued to the TV.

"Hey, Dad," she greeted, her voice ringing in her dad's ears.
"Hey, honey," Jeremy replied with a smile. "How was your first day?"
"It was good," Hannah responded, putting her plate of pizza and alfredo in the microwave. She sat down at the dining table, the soft hum of the microwave filling the kitchen. As she pulled her plate out, her phone buzzed, lighting up with a message from the group chat.

Zoey's text message appeared on the screen: *"I'm so happy I met you guys. We should hang out sometime."*

Hannah smiled, typing back, *"Me too. Thanks for making my first day a lot easier."*

A few seconds later, Sydney's text message with a happy emoji appeared. Feeling a surge of gratitude, Hannah liked the message, and Zoey quickly followed suit with her own "like."

After dinner, Hannah moved through her evening routine, settling into the comforting rhythm of getting ready for bed. However, there was still a lingering feeling that she couldn't shake off. She tried her best to push last night's nightmare aside. Just as she was about to climb into bed, a light knock echoed from her door.

"Come in," she called out.
Her mom poked her head into the room. "Hey," she said gently.

"Hey," said Hannah, her voice edged with weariness.

Maggie stepped fully into the room, her hands slowly pushing the door open. "I'm sorry I was late picking you up," she apologized. "My new job is keeping me busy."

Hannah smiled, her heart warmed by her mom's compassion. She loved her new school and was dying to share everything, but she could see the stress on her mom's face from her new job. "It's okay, Mom," she said, trying to lighten the mood. "At least you survived."

Maggie smiled gratefully, her tired expression easing. She leaned in and kissed Hannah on the cheek. "Thanks. I promise I'll be home earlier tomorrow. Goodnight," she said, her voice filled with humility.

"Goodnight, love you," said Hannah in a quiet voice.

Her mom smiled. "I love you, too," she said.

Hannah nodded silently as she watched her mom leave the room, softly closing the door behind her. She climbed into bed again, pulling the covers up to her shoulders, feeling the warmth of her sheets as she closed her eyes, hoping that a good night's sleep would slow her mind down from her first day. Suddenly, she felt the familiar visions returning to her as she tossed and turned. Her breath quickened while her palms began to sweat. She could feel the familiar tightness in her chest, the same eerie feeling that had plagued her every night.

CHAPTER 4

Hannah gasped sharply, her eyes snapping open as her body jolted awake. She blinked rapidly, her surroundings blurry and seemingly unfamiliar. She tried to make sense of it, but it was no use. She was standing in the middle of a dark forest. The trees crowded around her, branches swinging in the wind, reaching out like twisted fingers trying to imprison her. The branches grew closer and closer, as if the forest were alive. Her pulse quickened, her breathing becoming more shallow as she took a hesitant step back. Her bare foot crunched on the leaves below, and a chill ran down her spine.

"Hello?" she called out, her voice trembling as it echoed back. But the eerie silence ignored her calls, as if the forest refused to answer.

She felt helpless and alone, like in a cage she couldn't escape, as the silence closed in on her. Each step she took seemed to make the darkness grow heavier, the shadows wrapping around her, watching. Suddenly, a gust of wind blew through the trees, making Hannah shiver as she stumbled backward, fighting against the howling, swirling vortex. The air was sharply cold as it tried fiercely to carry her away. In the distance, she noticed a figure pulled away by the wind. The figure fought back against the relentless force but was shrouded in the swirling vortex, hardly visible throughout the storm.

It was a fairy queen, but not the same one from her vision. She collapsed, breathing heavily, her legs trembling as if they had almost given up on her. This fairy had tan skin, curly, chestnut hair, and brown eyes full of confusion and fear. She wore a beautiful tangerine-orange scoop neck, floor-length chiffon dress that shimmered in the moonlight, and a gold forehead diadem, its topaz glowing faintly in the center. However, her gradient wings—monarch and marigold-orange—caught Hannah's attention, glistening in the storm's turmoil.

Her heart skipped a beat as she stared into the fairy's elegant presence glimmering in the forest. Unexpectedly, her senses heightened as she noticed another figure hidden in the darkness. This one wore a black cloak with an iridescent pair of black and silver-blue wings. Hannah could feel an undeniable sense of danger as she felt the fairy's aura of ominous malice.

"Vivia?" the fairy queen called out, her voice trembling with fear and desperation.

The black-cloaked fairy's aura pulsed with an ominous energy. "Hello, Cecilia," she replied, her voice cold. "It's been a while."

Hannah saw the fear and anger in Cecilia's eyes, a flood of emotions she couldn't hide. "Why are you doing this?!" she demanded.

"After you, Aaron, and everyone else voted me for banishment, I decided everyone in the Avalon Forest had to go!" the black-cloaked fairy sneered. "First, I'll start with the rulers … starting with you."

Without warning, the two fairies collided in a fierce storm of magic. Vivia's dark, powerful magic surged forward like a hurricane, thick and menacing, while Cecilia countered with a radiant burst of orange magic, fierce and bright as the flaming sun. The air roared with raw power as their magic clashed, creating shockwaves in the forest. The ground and trees shook with vigorous authority, and the branches quivered wildly under the battle that raged above them. Despite the overwhelming odds, Cecilia didn't back down. She fought back with every ounce of strength, her every movement determined yet defiant.

Hannah's heart raced even more, torn between wanting to intervene to help Cecilia and the paralyzing fear that kept her frozen. All she could do was watch helplessly as the two fairies fought with magic after magic. With a final, explosive burst of energy, Vivia struck again, and Cecilia hit the floor with a loud thud. She groaned in pain, struggling to get up, but

Vivia's magic drained her strength. Seizing the moment, Vivia moved swiftly, brutally grabbing her wrist and stripping away her magic. Cecilia screamed in agony as her powers were drained, leaving her weak and defenseless.

"You and your beloved Aaron are no longer fit to rule the Topaz Kingdom, Cecilia," Vivia said, her eyes shining with malice. "It's time for me to take control of the Avalon Forest … and your precious kingdom. Soon, I will rule every kingdom in the Avalon Forest and the entire Avalon world. You will join the other kings and queens."

Despite the weariness in her body, Cecilia turned to face Vivia, her eyes burning with fierce defiance. "You'll … never … get away with this!" she shouted, her voice weak but still unwavering.

Vivia's smile grew colder and more callous as her eyes met Cecilia's gaze. "Oh, I already have," she said softly.

Hannah could no longer take it, feeling the adrenaline rushing through her veins, unleashing the courage she didn't know she had.

"Stop!" she screamed, her voice raw with desperation.
Without thinking, she ran toward the two fairies, focusing only on saving Cecilia and ending Vivia's reign of madness. Yet before she could reach them, two male dark fairies with gradient colors of black and red wings lunged and grabbed her. Their grips were as strong as iron as they held her back. Two female dark fairies with black and dark purple wings joined in as she struggled, almost blocking her view. She fought desperately to break free from their grasp, but their hands were too strong for her to handle. Panic flowed through her as she watched in horror, powerless to save Cecilia or prevent anything that was about to happen.

Vivia resumed her attention back to Cecilia, her eyes shining with more evil intent as she grabbed her wrist, this time with more brute force. Her blackish-purple aura glowed intensely as Cecilia's screams of desperation and fear echoed through the forest before being abruptly silenced. In an instant, Cecilia's body stiffened, her expression frozen in terror, and finally, she turned to stone.

"No!" Hannah screamed, her voice now filled with more desperation and dread.

Vivia's lips arched into a deadly smirk as she slowly turned to Hannah, her eyes glimmering with dark delight. A chill ran down Hannah's spine, and she swallowed hard. In the blink of an eye, Vivia's fairy form dissolved into a shadow—a black cloud of darkness that lunged toward her with enormous speed. Hannah tried to fight back, her body jerking with fear, but the dark fairies held her tightly, rendering her defenseless. She could feel the shadow's coldness closing in, suffocating her, creeping across her skin until…she woke up with a sharp gasp.

Her heart pounded violently in her chest as she sat upright in bed, quivering and breathing heavily as her eyes darted frantically around her room. Her hands trembled as they clutched tightly onto her seafoam green comforter, trying to calm herself. Everything was silent and still.

Suddenly, a creak of her bedroom door broke the silence. A scream of fear escaped from her lips as she instinctively scrambled away, her body tensing up as if preparing herself for a fight. Then her parents rushed in, concern written on their faces, and wrapped her in a tight embrace. Sadie quietly stood by the door, her worried expression fixed on Hannah.

"It's okay. It was just a nightmare," Maggie assured, her voice sympathetic and soothing.

Hannah clung to her parents, feeling the warmth of their presence and comfort. Her breathing finally calmed down, and her heart rate returned to normal. She felt her body relax, but the haunting images from her nightmares and visions continued to linger in her mind. She couldn't shake the feeling that something terrible was about to happen, though she couldn't put a finger on it. She pondered about Vivia and Cecilia, trying to understand who they were. Yet her mind lingered on why she was the only one who could see fairies. Her worries melted away as she drifted back into another peaceful slumber.

The next morning, Maggie hummed pleasantly as she poured orange juice into a glass. The sound of the liquid immersed the quiet kitchen. The aromas of buttermilk waffles, bacon, tomato, basil, and mozzarella frittatas filled the house, intertwining in the air. Hannah walked into the kitchen, wearing her mint green top with ruffled short sleeves and a round neckline. She paired it with light blue skinny jeans and white platform sneakers. She rubbed her eyes sleepily before her gaze drifted to her mom.

"Morning, Mom," she said, her voice low and weary.
Maggie smiled warmly, though a hint of concern lingered in her eyes, the weight from last night still pressing on her. "Good morning," she replied tenderly. "I…made you breakfast."

Hannah shook her head, glancing at the warm plate before her. "Thanks, but I'll stick with a Pop-Tart today," she said.

Hannah rummaged through the pantry, her fingers rushing past two cereal boxes until she pulled out a box of *Frosted Cookies & Crème Pop-Tarts*. After popping two into the toaster, she took a bite as soon as they finished. With her backpack slung over one shoulder, she glanced at her mom, who was eating her breakfast quietly, lost in her thoughts.

"Hey, uh … your father already left to take Sadie to school," Maggie said, watching Hannah pour herself a glass of apple juice. Hannah nodded, then watched her mom grab her briefcase.

"All right, you ready?" asked Maggie.
Hannah nodded subtly, grabbing her backpack again before heading toward the door. They quickly made their way to the car in silence, the engine's hum occupying the space between them. A twinge of guilt

washed over Hannah as they drove toward Avalon High. She couldn't shake the thought of how scared her family had been last night, knowing her nightmares would only add more to their worry.

"Mom, I'm sorry for scaring you, Dad, and Sadie last night," she said, breaking the silence in the car. "It was just a nightmare."

Maggie's right hand slipped from the steering wheel to squeeze her hand. "Hannah, if something is bothering you, you know you can always tell me," she said, her voice compassionate and reassuring.

Hannah let out a weary sigh and shook her head. She didn't want to burden her parents with her problems. "It's nothing, Mom," she said, trying to end the conversation. "Just a bad dream."

Maggie glanced at her daughter briefly, sensing that Hannah was hiding something behind the walls. However, she didn't press her. Maggie knew she would tell her when she was ready.

When the car stopped in front of the school, Hannah hastily unbuckled her seatbelt and stepped out. She quickly waved at her mom before heading toward the building and her second-period class, hoping to clear the lingering thoughts clouding her mind. As the school day went on, a gnawing feeling of uneasiness clung to her no matter how hard she tried to stay focused. Thankfully, her nightmares, flashbacks, and visions hadn't returned yet, but she could feel them lurking—waiting. She wasn't sure how long she could keep pretending everything was okay.

Finally, by the time sixth period rolled around, Hannah felt temporarily relieved. Mr. Snyder's laid-back, easygoing personality and his jokes helped her forget about her nightmares and visions, only for a little while. In fact, she was surprised to find herself laughing at one of his jokes. Mr. Snyder waited patiently until the conversations in the classroom quieted down, then looked around before starting the lesson.

"Okay, guys, I need you to get into groups of two or three," he said. Hannah scanned the room as the students started to move around, trying to find a group to join. She hesitated for a moment before approaching one desk, but the moment she did, a pair of students glanced at her while one of them turned away. Hannah moved to the next group, feeling overlooked. Again, she was met with a courteous but firm exclusion. She continued to move, growing more alone with each rejection. Mr. Snyder, noticing Hannah still standing alone, observed her with quiet concern as she searched for a group.

"Hey, Hannah, why don't you join these two over at the top right corner of the room?" he said, gesturing toward two girls in the corner, chatting in low voices.

Hannah looked to the back right corner of the room, where two girls were sitting. She immediately recognized the Hispanic girl from yesterday—the one who commented on her necklace. Today, she wore a medium blue jean jacket over a gray short-sleeved V-neck top and dark blue skinny jeans. Her gray lace-up high-top sneakers completed her look.

The other girl, whom she hadn't met before, immediately caught her attention. With light skin and hazel eyes seemingly glistening in the light, she stood at about 5'10"—taller than both Hannah and the Hispanic girl.

Her blonde hair was styled in two neat fishtail braids, though a few strands softly framed her face. She wore a dark gray, long-sleeved scoop-neck knit top, a black skater skirt, and sleek black knee-high boots. Her style was similar to the Hispanic girl's—girly, sophisticated, and trendy but with a more chic, modern, polished, preppy, and refined twist.

"All right, I want the left side of the room to discuss ancient Asia while the right side discusses ancient Egypt," Mr. Snyder said. "You have thirty minutes. Have fun!"

Everyone gathered around, engaging in their conversations as they settled in. Hannah turned to the Hispanic girl sitting next to her. "Hey, uh … you mentioned my necklace yesterday, right?" she asked, her voice barely a whisper.

The Hispanic girl looked at her, briefly puzzled, but then her eyes landed on Hannah's necklace.

"Oh yeah, I saw you in the cafeteria," she said, her voice friendly and honest. "It looked really cute with your outfit."

The blonde-haired girl took her eyes off her notebook, lingering on Hannah's necklace for a second. She bit her lip and shifted in her seat before she spoke. Her voice was barely a whisper. "Oh yeah, that looks so good with your shirt," she said.

Hannah's face blossomed with a big smile, her eyes lighting up. "Thanks, I'm Hannah," she replied, her voice upbeat and friendly.

The Hispanic girl's lips curved into a grin. "I'm Dominique," she introduced herself. "But you can call me Dom."

The blonde-haired girl spoke again, her voice meek as her eyes rapidly drifted back to the necklace. "I'm Amber," she said, her tone hesitant, almost like she was still deciding whether to speak. She paused, her gaze lingering on the necklace for a little longer, her brow creased in a hint of curiosity. "Did you know that I have the same necklace?"

Hannah blinked in disbelief. She thought that she, Sydney, and Zoey shared the same necklace—each unique with different birthstones and zodiac signs. To her surprise, Dominique's expression mirrored her own: shocked, wide-eyed, and filled with the same confusion.

Amber pulled out her necklace, her fingers brushing the cool charms as she revealed it to Hannah. The necklace was nearly identical to Hannah's, except for the aquamarine and the golden Pisces sign hanging from it.

"My birthstone's an aquamarine," she explained with a trace of a smile. "I've had this necklace since the day I was born."

Just as Hannah was about to respond, Dominique surprised them both by reaching under her shirt and pulling out her necklace. Its design was almost identical to theirs. Instead of an emerald or aquamarine, it featured a sapphire and a golden Virgo symbol dangling beneath it. "Mine's a sapphire," she explained, her voice steady. "I was born on September 21st. I've been wearing it since I was born, too. Did you know that sapphires stand for sincerity and truth? Aquamarines represent youth and happiness, and emeralds symbolize loyalty and peace."

Hannah was in awe. She'd never seen anything like it before. She wondered if anyone else was wearing the same necklace as Sydney, Zoey, Dominique, Amber, or her.

"When's your guys' birthday?" Dominique asked, her eyes sparking with curiosity.

"Mine's March 10th," Amber answered.
"Mine's May 15th," Hannah added, smiling shyly.
Amber's eyes flickered as her smile widened. "Yay, we're spring month buddies!" she cheered, her voice bubbling enthusiastically.

Dominique and Hannah exchanged surprised glances. They had always thought Amber was a shy, quiet girl who kept to herself. As she noticed their wide-eyed reactions, Amber's cheeks flushed pink. She quickly lowered her gaze, her voice quieting. "Um … " she murmured.

Hannah and Dominique couldn't help but smile at her shy response, realizing there was more to Amber than they had first thought. After a few moments, the bell rang, signaling the end of sixth-period class with a sharp sound. All the students grabbed their backpacks and chatted excitedly as they headed out the door into the busy hallway.

"Okay, guys, be sure to read chapter two and be ready to discuss it for Monday's class," Mr. Snyder called out, his voice carrying across the room. "Then, we'll dive into the Western River Valley Civilization. Have a good weekend!"

Hannah, Dominique, and Amber grabbed their backpacks and left the classroom, the hall bustling with students heading to their next class. As they walked down the hall, Dominique turned to Hannah. "Hey, have you met anyone yet?" she asked.

"Um, I just made friends with two people yesterday," said Hannah, her voice a little unsure but still upbeat.

Dominique grinned as she pulled out her phone. "Well, consider me your third!" she said cheerfully.

Hannah and Dominique exchanged phone numbers, Instagram handles, and Snapchat usernames. When Dominique scrolled through Hannah's Instagram, she giggled kindly when she paused on one post—a drawing of a fairy flying over the water.

"So, you're the artsy type, huh?" she asked.
"Yeah, I usually post my drawings on Instagram, especially fairies, pegasi, and sprites," Hannah replied, her cheeks flushed in embarrassment. "I guess my friends from my old school didn't share the same interests as mine. Is that weird?"

"Not at all!" Dominique said, letting out a warm, reassuring smile. "I think having friends with different, unique interests is cool."

Hannah's heart lifted as she returned the smile, feeling like she had found a new friend who truly understood her. Amber, who had been quietly observing the exchange, suddenly handed her phone to Hannah, revealing her Instagram page for Dominique and her to see.

"Here's mine," she said, her voice becoming a little louder.
Hannah and Dominique exchanged phone numbers, Instagram handles, and Snapchat usernames with Amber, smiling and happy to have made new friendships. After saying goodbye to Dominique and Amber, Hannah turned toward her last class—Chemistry I.

She navigated through the crowded hallway, the clatter of footsteps around her, but a sense of relief slowly washed over her. Meeting Dominique and Amber helped her ease the anxiety significantly that had been weighing on her all day, especially her nightmares and visions. Still, her mind couldn't stop reverting to the necklace. It felt like a strange coincidence that her necklace was identical to Sydney's, Zoey's, Dominique's, and Amber's—just with different birthstones and different zodiac signs. She wondered who else had that same necklace and why it felt so important.

Her thoughts were interrupted when someone bumped into her, knocking her schedule out of her hands. She quickly stopped to pick it up, her eyes glancing at the person colliding with her. The girl was African American, with dark brown hair and brown skin that matched her brown eyes. She stood about 5'6", just a bit shorter than Hannah. She had a tomboyish vibe, like Sydney, Zoey, and her, but with a girly flair. Her style leaned more toward the urban, sporty side. She wore deep blue overalls over a yellow V-neck tee and matching yellow low-top sneakers.

"I'm sorry, I didn't see you," the girl apologized quickly, bending down to help pick up Hannah's schedule.

"It's okay, don't worry about it," Hannah replied, grabbing her schedule from the girl's hands.

The girl smiled back, her expression friendly. "I'm Nia, by the way. I just came from Spanish class," she said.

"I'm Hannah. I was actually heading to Hamilton's class," Hannah replied.

"Oh, that's where I'm going too! But you're going the wrong way, though," Nia chuckled, tilting her head in the opposite direction.

Hannah let out a small laugh at herself, followed by a murmured "Oh." "Don't worry, it happens!" Nia said, leading the way to their chemistry class.

As they walked, Hannah's curiosity got the better of her. "So, what's Hamilton like?" she asked.

Nia's face lit up as she spoke. "Well, *Mrs.* Hamilton is one of the new teachers," she said. "She's super knowledgeable, kind, and supportive. She's very sweet—always pleasant, friendly, and helpful. She's very direct and gets straight to the point. She's also extremely easy to talk to and is always willing to help if you get stuck on something."

"Wow, she sounds like a great teacher," Hannah commented.
"She is. She's the real deal," Nia replied, her cheerful smile widening. "She's so fun and makes chemistry class enjoyable for all of us. You're going to love her."

Hannah's excitement grew as she nodded eagerly. "That's amazing," she said, feeling more excited about the class.

Nia chuckled softly at Hannah's remark. "As long as you understand that she's the class star, you'll be just fine, and you'll get an A," she said. "Mrs. Hamilton is amazing. Her passion for chemistry and unique teaching style make the class so fun. That's why science is my favorite class, and she's already my favorite teacher. She's not just a great teacher—she's like a mother figure to all of us. She's so caring and sincerely understands everyone's different situations. She's just an all-around awesome teacher."

Hannah's excitement flickered to life as she listened to Nia's words. Mrs. Hamilton sounded phenomenal, and how Nia's face lit up made her eager to meet the teacher. Nia's energy was so contagious, almost humming in the air. Without even realizing it, Hannah felt a smile tug at her lips. The brightly charged energy seemed to fill the space between them. Nia's bubbly, playful, carefree spirit was impossible to ignore. She was so sweet, cheerful, and full of life. Her upbeat personality made everything brighter.

 A glimmer of recognition flashed as Nia's eyes looked down on Hannah's necklace. "You know, I have that same necklace!" she grinned. "I always wear it every day."

Hannah's eyes widened in surprise. "Really?" she asked, her heart skipping a beat. "Are you a Taurus?"

Nia shook her head, still smiling. "Nope! I'm a Libra. My birthday's October 18th," she said.

"You're kidding?" Hannah exclaimed, blinking in disbelief.
Nia laughed and shook her head, another playful sparkle in her eyes. "Nope," she said, pulling her necklace over her shirt. It was just like Hannah's, but with a pink tourmaline and a golden Libra sign dangling from it.

"Wow, that's amazing," Hannah said. "I was born on May 15th."
As they entered the classroom, Hannah and Nia immediately spotted Mrs. Hamilton's smile. It was warm and inviting, a smile that made the room less intimidating. Around them, a sea of unfamiliar faces filled the room, except for Dominique and Amber. A wave of relief washed over her, the warmth of familiar faces easing her nerves. But when her eyes scanned the rest of the room, her stomach sank as she spotted Heather and Carleigh. She wasn't ready for them since their chilly encounter yesterday.

Hannah couldn't help but admire Mrs. Hamilton's striking appearance. Her beautiful brown skin seemed to illuminate under the afternoon sunlight, and her wavy black hair flowed down in soft waves, streaked with ombre honey-blonde highlights that shimmered with every movement. Her warm brown eyes sparkled when she smiled. She wore a burgundy V-neck button-down blouse with pockets, black leggings, and black chunky ankle boots. Like Ms. Reza, Mrs. Hamilton had that effortless style, confidence, and warmth that made her seem approachable and easy to talk to.

"Hi, you must be Hannah Sumpter," said Mrs. Hamilton. Hannah smiled modestly and nodded as she walked to the fourth row, sitting at an empty desk. "Good afternoon, everyone!" Mrs. Hamilton's voice rang out, passionate and welcoming. "Before I take attendance, we have a new student today. Please welcome Hannah Sumpter to our class. She's from Chicago. Hannah, meet the entire seventh-period class!"

The room erupted into chatter as students turned to her. Some called out friendly hellos, while others offered shy smiles, nodded, or merely waved. Hannah responded to each greeting with an unassuming smile or a low wave. Slowly, the noise settled down. Mrs. Hamilton finished taking attendance and turned to the other students, her expression welcoming. "Okay, I want everyone to get into groups of four," she began.

The other students quickly moved to form their groups, rushing to the back to find their tables, but Hannah was left standing alone again, just like in Mr. Snyder's class. Her eyes darted around the room, unsure of where to go, feeling the familiar weight of being left out. Mrs. Hamilton, noticing her hesitation, stepped out from behind her desk with a kind smile. "Hannah, you can join Nia's group," she said, gesturing toward the trio sitting together at a table in the front row.

A beam of solace washed over Hannah as she nodded, grateful for Mrs. Hamilton's kindness. She made her way to the front row, her steps a little slower than usual, but the sight of Nia, Amber, and Dominique made her feel a little lighter. A smile spread across her face, happy to be with their familiar faces again.

"All right, we all know what solubility is, right? Does anyone remember what it is?" said Mrs. Hamilton, her voice firm but carrying a singsong quality. "We talked about this on Tuesday."

No one said a word until Dominique raised her hand, smiling with glee. "It means a substance that can dissolve in a solvent, particularly water," she answered.

Hannah, Amber, and Nia exchanged surprised glances at Dominique's quick and insightful answer. It was clear that Dominique had a fierce passion for chemistry, her voice practically bubbling with excitement.

"That is correct, Dominique," said Mrs. Hamilton. "Now, what about a suspension? Anyone?"

Dominique raised her hand again, but Nia was quicker, her hand shooting up first. "A suspension is a combination of liquid and solid particles," said Nia.

"Yes, Nia," Mrs. Hamilton replied with a smile.
Dominique felt a twinge of competition twisting in her stomach as Nia answered first, but she quickly pushed it aside, forcing her face into a composed, neutral expression. She hid any signs of jealousy, not wanting Nia, Hannah, or Amber to notice.

"Okay, now that we learned about solubility and suspensions, let's put our knowledge to the test," Mrs. Hamilton said, her voice full of exhilaration. "For today's activity, we will experiment with the reactions between salt and water. We have iodized salt, garlic salt, sea salt, and Himalayan pink salt. Now, each of you will take one type of salt and put it into a separate cup labeled A, B, C, or D. After that, you will write down and explain why each salt reacts the way it does in the water."

CHAPTER 5

The room hummed with students talking and scribbling notes as the class continued. Dominique stood up, her shoes squeaking softly against the floor as she left to get the sea salt at the supply table. She carefully grabbed a clear cup of sea salt, its small, visible cube-shaped particles settling like tiny crystals at the bottom. With a steady hand, she poured the salt into another cup labeled "C," sprinkling with the serene hush of a distant whisper. Meanwhile, Amber turned to Nia, her expression a mixture of curiosity and recognition.

"Hey, aren't you in my second-period class with Ms. Reza?" she asked. "Oh right, I am," Nia said, her face brightening with enthusiasm. "Did you get through chapters three, four, and five of *The Great Gatsby*?"

Amber nodded back, her curiosity piqued. "Yeah, what did you think of it?" she asked.

When Dominique returned, Hannah listened intently as Nia shared her thoughts on *The Great Gatsby*. Dominique poured the sea salt into the water, sinking with a soft swirl. The salt quickly dissolved, turning the once-clear water into a slightly cloudy liquid. Tiny bubbles rose to the surface like the water was coming alive. She then explained the reaction as the others took notes. After they were done, Nia's eyes sprang open in surprise when she noticed Dominique's and Amber's necklaces.

"Wait ... " she said, pointing at their necklaces. "You guys are wearing the same necklace as me."

Amber and Dominique exchanged a glance, both smiling. "Yeah, but my birthstone's a sapphire, and I'm a Virgo," Dominique explained, pointing to her gemstone.

"Mine's an aquamarine, and I'm a Pisces," Amber added, showing off her gemstone with a grin.

Nia's smile stretched radiantly. "That's so cool! I'm a Libra, and my birthstone's a tourmaline," she said, proudly showing off her necklace.

"Person D, it's your turn to get the Himalayan pink salt," Mrs. Hamilton said, interrupting their conversation.

Hannah stood up from her group and walked over to the supply table. As she reached for the Himalayan pink salt, she felt something shift in the room. She looked up, her eyes meeting Heather's gaze, sending a chill down her spine. Heather's eyes narrowed, a smug smirk creeping onto the corners of her lips. Tension was in the air, but Hannah didn't flinch. She scoffed, rolling her eyes, and calmly turned back toward her group without a word. Hannah wasn't interested in getting involved with Heather and her drama. She had better things to do.

Suddenly, a piercing scream cut through the room. Everyone turned to see Heather's beautiful white V-neck sleeveless shirt with ruffle details, now drenched in Himalayan salt water. The fabric clung to her skin, completely soaked. Heather's fists clenched at her sides, her body trembling with barely contained fury. Her face twisted into a furious scowl.

"My shirt! It cost $200!" Heather screeched, glaring around the classroom. "Who did this?! Who is responsible for ruining my shirt?!"

The silent tension hung, thickening and settling like a storm cloud. No one said a word, not even Heather's group members. They stared at her with wide eyes, frozen in place. Heather's anger bubbled, seething even more as her fists clenched tighter. "No one's gonna fess up?!" she snapped, her voice sharp and full of outrage.

Again, no one spoke. The silence was overbearing until Carleigh suddenly pointed at Hannah, her finger accusing. "It was obviously Hannah," she said. "I saw her do it on purpose."

Hannah's eyes flew open, her jaw hanging open as her face twisted in disbelief. "What? I would never do something like that," she screeched, her face red with fury as she stormed toward Heather and Carleigh. "How dare you?!"

Hannah, Heather, and Carleigh were locked in a shouting match, their loud voices echoing off the classroom walls. Words flew back and forth, accusation after accusation. Their faces grew redder with every insult shooting through the air like arrows. Just as the chaos reached a boiling point, Mrs. Hamilton walked over, her face set in a stern, no-nonsense expression. The sharp click of her boots reverberated against the floor, cutting through the noise with each step she took. As she drew closer, her presence silenced the shouting.

"What is all of this commotion?" she demanded, her voice firm.
"Mrs. Hamilton," Heather shrieked. "Hannah ruined my $200 shirt with Himalayan salt water."

"She's lying! I didn't do it!" Hannah screamed, her hands waving in frustration.

Heather's mouth dropped, ready to throw more accusations, but before she could say anything else, a student with sandy brown hair and green eyes from Heather's group stepped forward. Her expression was serious. Her brow tightened in confusion as she glanced at Heather and Carliegh.

"Mrs. Hamilton, I overheard Heather and Carleigh talking about embarrassing Hannah," she said, her voice low but firm, disbelief lacing her words. "They were planning to spill the water on Heather's shirt and blame it on her."

Mrs. Hamilton's expression shifted as she quickly processed the words, her brow furrowing in disbelief. After a sharp intake of breath, her skepticism subsided. She glanced at Heather, narrowing her eyes at the shocked look on Heather's face.

"Are you seriously gonna believe her?!" Heather shrieked, her voice full of fury.

Mrs. Hamilton pointed toward the door, her sharp eyes locking with Heather's. "Actually, I am," she said, her tone cutting, leaving no room for argument. "Go to Ms. Caldwell's office."

Heather opened her mouth to argue, but Mrs. Hamilton cut her off with a glare, silencing her instantly. Murmurs of shock rippled through the intense, heavy silence as everyone watched Heather snatch her belongings. She stormed out, not before casting one last intimidating glare at Hannah, who met her relentless stare without flinching. A stunned and defeated Carleigh slowly shuffled back to her seat, her head hanging low as her shoulders slumped. Hannah exhaled a deep sigh of relief, her shoulders relaxing as the turmoil eased. Mrs. Hamilton turned to her, her expression softening as she offered a small, comforting smile.

"Don't let Heather or Carleigh get under your skin, okay?" she said, her voice calm and reassuring. "If it happens again, let me know."

Hannah smiled back, a sense of ease from Mrs. Hamilton washing over her. Exhaling deeply, she then turned and made her way back to her group.

"All right, everyone, back to work," said Mrs. Hamilton.
Dominique turned to Hannah, her brow knitted with worry. "Hey, you okay?" she asked, her voice gentle.

Hannah smiled at the other girls, feeling the relief settle in after dealing with more of Heather's shenanigans. "I am now," she said.

Nia nudged Hannah's shoulder lightly with a grin. "What you did out there was amazing," she said admiringly. "You showed Heather that you're not playing any games."

A warm feeling spread through Hannah as she looked at her friends, her smile growing. As soon as the bell rang, the classroom came alive with the clamor of zipping backpacks and papers shoved into bags filling the classroom. Chatter and conversations wafted in the air as students filed out one by one.

"Have a good weekend, everyone!" Mrs. Hamilton called out.
As Hannah stepped out of the classroom, her eyes immediately found Dominque, Nia, and Amber leaning against the lockers, chatting and laughing. Nia grinned at her, waving as she reached into her pink and black checkered backpack and pulled out her car keys. The initial "N" sparkled in the light as they jingled while hanging from a soft blush pink tassel keychain. The keys bounced along with a fluffy pink pom-pom keychain with the word "Dance" embroidered in bold magenta letters.

"Ready to start the weekend?" asked Dominique, her voice a mixture of weariness and excitement.

Nia's grin spread broadly, her eyes sparkling. "I can't wait for the weekend!" she said.

Hannah couldn't help but smile, shaking her head in disbelief. "I still can't believe Mrs. Hamilton stuck up for me," she said, her eyes enlarged with surprise. "I thought I was gonna get in trouble."

Nia nudged Hannah again, a playful grin spreading across her face. "I told you she's very understanding," she said. "Once you get to know her, you'll be her best friend. Like I said, she's the real deal."

Genuine smiles lit up the faces of the other girls as they laughed. They were all beginning to unwind and enjoy Nia's company without realizing it because her energy seemed to light up the room. It was easy to be around her, and they were immediately glad to have someone like her in their group.

Hannah turned to Nia, pausing for a moment before offering a smile. "Do you wanna exchange phone numbers or something?" she asked.

"Yeah, it would be cool to stay in touch," Amber said.
Nia's face lit up instantly, her eyes sparkling. "Yeah, come on," she said, her voice brimming with excitement.

The four girls quickly swapped phone numbers, Instagram handles, and Snapchat handles, their fingers gliding across the screen as they laughed and chatted.

"We can work out some time," Nia said. "I heard about a new coffee shop we could try at the Avalon Open Air Mall."

Dominique, quiet throughout the conversation, reached into her denim laptop backpack and pulled out her car keys. She held them up. Her keychains caught the light with the flags of Colombia, Venezuela, El Salvador, and Mexico. A glinting blue rhinestone heart glimmered softly.

"I would love to join you guys!" she exclaimed. "I'm a total shopaholic, so this is right up my alley."

Amber's grin grew as she shyly tugged the sleeve of her shirt. "Me too!" she said, her mellow voice rising cheerfully. "I can't wait to go shopping and try that new coffee shop."

Nia's smile lingered as her foot turned in the opposite direction. "Well, I better get going. Catch you guys later!" she said, waving as she walked away.

The girls said their goodbyes and went their separate ways. Hannah felt her phone vibrate in her pocket as she walked down the stairs. She pulled it out, her eyes landing on a text from her mom:

"On my way. At QuikTrip getting some gas," the text read.

As Hannah was about to prepare to text her mom, someone called out, "Ms. Sumpter," ringing in her ears. She turned around to see Heather standing next to a woman.

Hannah blinked, taken aback by the woman's striking appearance. Her honey-blonde hair fell in cascading waves around her face, and her piercing green eyes sparkled with confidence and kindness. She had fair skin and was dressed in a bright purple pencil dress paired with black dress sandals, looking both stylish and professional at the same time.

"Hi, you must be Hannah," said the woman, her smile beaming warmly. "I'm Mrs. Barringer, one of the guidance counselors."

Hannah couldn't help but notice how Mrs. Barringer's smile was bright and genuine, her voice kind and inviting. Heather stood off to the side with her arms crossed. Her eyes looked away as if deliberately avoiding eye contact, her expression distant and uninterested.

"I'm sorry to bother you," Mrs. Barringer said, her smile faltering for a second. "But I was wondering if I could have a minute of your time to discuss something regarding my daughter, Heather."

Hannah's eyes widened in surprise. She could hardly believe that she was meeting Heather's mom for the first time, and learning that Mrs. Barringer was one of the guidance counselors made her stomach churn. Her heart sank, feeling a sudden rush of uneasiness, thinking if she'd done something wrong. Before she could speak, Mrs. Barringer beat her to it, bringing up the chemistry incident.

"I'll get straight to the point," Mrs. Barringer said, her voice gentle but firm. "I heard about what happened between you, Heather, and her friend Carleigh in chemistry class with Mrs. Hamilton. I want to apologize on behalf of Heather for her behavior. I have a feeling that she owes you an apology as well."

Hannah froze, caught off guard by Mrs. Barringer's words. "No, it's okay. I don't want to cause any trouble," she said, quickly shaking her head.

Mrs. Barringer did not back down, arms crossed, not moving an inch. She looked at Heather consistently and without flinching. "Heather," she insisted. "I think it's time for you to make things right with Hannah."

Heather rolled her eyes, letting out a sharp scoff as her mom's words hung heavy. Hannah could see the irritation in her stiff posture by the way she crossed her arms again. "Fine," she huffed, finally glancing at Hannah. "I'm sorry for what happened in chemistry class. It was all a stupid prank, and I'm sorry I dragged you into it."

Hannah's eyes popped, blinking rapidly. She couldn't believe it. Heather was *actually* apologizing, but it didn't feel real. The words didn't match the look on her face or how she'd acted before. Something inside Hannah shifted. She knew that she couldn't trust her one bit. She had to speak up or do something. If Heather kept this up, she wouldn't let it slide.

"It's okay," she mumbled, shrugging her shoulders, not wanting to cause any more trouble.

Mrs. Barringer smiled, her hands gently patting both of their shoulders. "That's better," she said warmly. "Now, why don't you two become friends? I have a feeling you'll get along just fine."

Hannah felt a wave of skepticism, but didn't want to argue in front of Heather's mom. She gave a quick nod, offering a goodbye to Mrs. Barringer. As she walked away, Hannah bit her lip, letting the nagging feeling stay with her. She was unable to get rid of the persistent uneasiness. Although grateful that Mrs. Barringer had forced an apology out of Heather, Heather's intense glare made it clear that Hannah needed to be cautious and keep her distance from the mean girl. After meeting with Sydney and Zoey, she wasted no time explaining everything.

"Wait, so Mrs. Barringer is Heather's mom, and she *actually* forced her to apologize?" Sydney asked, her eyes gaping in shock.

"That's not all," Hannah said. "Heather and Carleigh were trying to set me up with the salt water incident until Mrs. Hamilton defended me and sent Heather to the principal's office."

"It's a good thing I have Mrs. Hamilton for sixth period," said Zoey, chuckling as she swept a strand of hair behind her ear.

Sydney's brows clenched together, and she cleared her throat. "Um, Zoey? We both have Mrs. Hamilton for sixth period," she said.

"Oh right," Zoey replied, rolling her eyes. "I forgot about that."
The girls giggled at Zoey's moment of forgetfulness.
"Hey, are you guys free this Saturday?" Sydney asked, shifting the conversation.

"I was planning on doing some homework," said Zoey. "Why do you ask?"

"Well, my mom has to work the twelve-hour shift, my dad's doing overtime, and my sister, Kennedy, is going to a party," Sydney said, her voice trailing off with excitement. "So, I was wondering if you guys wanna come to my house for a sleepover?"

Hannah and Zoey exchanged surprised glances. Neither of them had ever been to a sleepover before, and the thought of spending the night with Sydney sounded exciting.

"I'd love to!" Hannah exclaimed.
"Count me in!" Zoey said, her voice bubbling with anticipation. "I've never been to a sleepover before."

Sydney's face lit up, her enthusiasm practically jumping out of her. "Don't worry, it's going to be so much fun," she said. "I'll text you the details later."

Just then, Hannah's eyes caught a glimpse of her mom's car pulling into the school parking lot. She quickly said goodbye to Sydney and Zoey before hurrying to the car. Hannah explained Sydney's invitation to a sleepover to her mom as soon as she got in.

"Who's Sydney?" Maggie asked, her eyebrow raised in curiosity. Hannah's face lit up with a smile. "She's the girl who's been helping me with my classes," she explained. "We even have a few classes together."

Her mom smiled tenderly. "That's great," she asked, her tone full of interest. "Do you know what you'll take to the sleepover?"

Hannah thought for a moment, considering her words. "I was thinking about bringing some cupcakes," she replied.

Maggie nodded enthusiastically, her smile inviting. "Sounds good," she said, her voice cheerful and supportive. "We can buy some cupcakes tomorrow before the sleepover."

Hannah's face lit up with enthusiasm. It was finally happening—her very first sleepover! She couldn't wait to spend more time with her new friends outside of school. Staying up late made her heart race with joy and exhilaration.

When Hannah and Maggie got home, Hannah checked her phone and saw a text from Sydney with the details:

"Here's the address: 212 Chestnut Ave. Avalon, MO, 64186. It starts at 5:45 p.m. on Saturday. Can't wait!" the text message read.

Hannah smiled and showed her mom the text message. Maggie gave her a quick nod. "Okay, we'll head out at the right time," she said, a smile curving across her lips.

By 4:30 p.m. on Saturday, warm golden colors painted the sky as the sun started to set. Hannah zipped up her teal duffle bag, ready for the night ahead. She stuffed the last of her things in her teal duffle bag, double-checking she had everything she needed for the night. She wore her cozy, jade green, long-sleeved crewneck pajama top and dark green joggers. Slipping on her white cross-band slippers, she pulled her hair into a neat middle-part ponytail.

After she packed, Hannah grabbed her seafoam green sleeping bag and headed to the kitchen. Maggie followed her in to help. Together, they carefully picked up the cupcake container and ensured it was secure. They walked out the door and climbed into the car with the cupcakes safely in hand. Maggie set the directions on the GPS, letting the screen blink, and then the estimated time and directions flashed.

"Forty-five minutes," she murmured, glancing over at Hannah with a grin. "We'll be there before you know it."

The drive felt smooth, the houses passing by as they made their way to Sydney's house. When they finally arrived, Hannah's eyes brightened with anticipation. Sydney's house looked so different from hers. It had a modern, contemporary design with a brown exterior, giving it a polished but inviting look. The dark, earthy tones of its smooth, sleek wood were accented by crisp white and gray trim. Sydney's car was parked neatly on the left side of the garage. A limestone walkway framed by tall windows led up to the front door. Hannah stepped out of the car, grabbing her duffle bag, sleeping bag, and the container of cupcakes.

"Have fun!" Maggie called out before driving off.
Taking a deep breath, Hannah knocked three times. The music drifted from inside, the bass banging softly against the door as the rhythm pulsed rapidly. Sydney opened the door, wearing a sky-blue satin short-sleeved button-down pajama top decorated with delicate maple leaf patterns and matching shorts. She completed the look with comfy orange plaid scuff

shoes. Her hair hung loose around her shoulders, adding to her cozy, relaxed vibe.

"You made it!" Sydney exclaimed, her face illuminating with a wide grin. The two girls rushed to give each other a quick hug, unable to contain their joy.

After Sydney took Hannah's cupcakes, she ushered her inside. Hannah paused for a minute, taking in the beauty of Sydney's home. Ahead of her, the white hallway lengthened, its creamy white walls lined with velvety, rich tones. A set of wooden quarter-turned stairs with brown, refined banisters curved upward at the end of the hall. Framed pictures of Sydney and her family smiled down from the walls, capturing their happiest moments. The space was stunning and inviting, with taupe walls giving a modern yet peaceful atmosphere.

The kitchen embodied a contemporary charm. The silver fridge stood proudly against the wall, letting the polished surface carry through the light. Above, the arched cabinets were a warm, rich shade of brown, their smooth contours providing a sophisticated yet cozy space. The stainless steel oven reflected under the soft, hollowed lights. Hannah's eyes wandered over the granite countertops, their smooth surface glinting in the light. She noticed the neatly organized kitchen drawers and the large pantry off to the side, its wooden doors slightly open.

As she ventured toward the living room, she noticed the black sectional couch neatly positioned in front of an oval-shaped oak coffee table, its smooth surface reflecting the light. In the far corner, a round white pedestal dining table stood, its glossy surface gently gleaming in the warm glow, surrounded by four white solid-back chairs that completed the look.

Then, as Hannah placed her seafoam green sleeping bag in the living room corner, she spotted the familiar faces of Zoey, Dominique, Amber, Nia, and Rachelle, all sitting on the couch, chatting and laughing lively together.

Zoey wore a black short-sleeved pajama tee, purple fleece shorts, and matching purple memory foam loafer slippers. Her hair fell loose around her shoulders, and her grape purple sleeping bag spread out beside her. With her high half ponytail, Dominique wore a lake blue satin short-sleeved button-down pajama shirt and matching shorts. Her navy faux fur-lined slide shoes completed her look, and her sapphire-blue sleeping bag lay next to Zoey's.

Amber wore a beige cotton long-sleeved pajama shirt and plush matching flannel pants. Her chestnut-colored, fluffy winter house shoes kept her warm, and she styled her hair in two ponytails—half up and half down. Her cyan sleeping bag rested on Dominique's.

Nia wore a wine-red satin long-sleeved button-down pajama shirt and matching shorts with her black faux-fur-lined slide shoes. She tied her hair into a mid-ponytail, and her bubblegum-pink sleeping bag was beside Dominique's.

Last but not least, Rachelle wore a white cotton flannel long-sleeved pajama shirt and pants with pink polka dots. She wore cozy winter slip-on house shoes, and her hair was loose. Her light pink sleeping bag was next to Nia's.

Hannah's eyes sparked with surprise at seeing them all together in one place. A big smile spread across her face as she hurried over to the couch, practically bursting with joy. "What are you guys doing here?" she asked.

"Sydney invited us," Nia explained eagerly, her eyes sparkling with exhilaration. "Since we all have the same Culinary Arts class together."

Sydney set the cupcakes on the dining table, adding to the spread of pizza, ice cream, cookies, and other delicious treats. She grabbed her tangerine orange sleeping bag and spread it out in the corner of the living room beside Hannah's.

The girls played games, laughed, danced, and snacked endlessly as the night went on. They lounged on the couch, enjoying each other's company, not a care in the world. Their lively laughter and conversation filled the house, echoing through every corner. Music played loudly in the background, changing from one artist to the next, each new song adding to the fun. As the sun slipped beneath the horizon, dusk turned to night, the golden colors fading into the shades of purple and dark blue.

Hannah walked into the kitchen, grabbed a plate, and gathered graham crackers, chocolate, and marshmallows to make her s'mores. Outside on the patio, Zoey, Dominique, Amber, Nia, and Rachelle were gathered around a gray concrete fire pit, the warm, faint glow flickering across their faces as they relaxed on the comfortable gray sectional seating group with cushions. Suddenly, the sliding door creaked open, and Rachelle stepped inside, her footsteps slow and heavy. She looked pale. Her face tightened with discomfort. Her phone was pressed to her right ear, but she wasn't just speaking. She groaned meekly as she winced, one hand clutching her stomach tightly. She took another slow step forward, dragging her feet.

Hannah's brow drew inward as she walked over to Rachelle. "Hey, you okay?" she asked, her voice full of concern. She gently rubbed Rachelle's back, her touch warm and comforting as she waited for her response.

Rachelle shook her head, her face slightly twisting more in pain. "I don't feel so good," she whimpered. "I think my stomach hurts. I called my mom to see if she was on her way."

Hannah's eyes filled with concern as she watched Rachelle wince. "If you like, I can call my mom to see if she can drive you home," she offered, her hand resting on Rachelle's shoulder.

Rachelle shook her head weakly, her voice barely audible through the pain. "I'll be okay …" she said, forcing a smile that didn't quite reach her eyes. "My mom's already on her way."

Just then, Sydney came down the stairs, holding a box of game cards labeled *How Well Do You Know Your Best Friends?* "Hey! I've got a fun game for us to play! You guys are gonna love it," she grinned, her excitement contagious.

Hannah nodded enthusiastically, though a shadow of concern persisted for Rachelle. She went back into the kitchen to grab her plate. But when she returned, she and Sydney saw Rachelle heading out the door, still looking unwell. They exchanged worried glances but moved on with the night, hoping Rachelle would feel better soon. They headed outside, where Zoey, Dominique, Amber, and Nia were already soaking in the heat of the fire, roasting marshmallows, their chatter and laughter echoing in the quiet night.

As they enjoyed their s'mores, Dominique glanced around from side to side, her brows gathered in thought. "Hey, where's Rachelle?" she asked, her voice laced with curiosity.

Sydney shrugged, a hint of remorse crossing her face. "She wasn't feeling too well, so she had to head home early," she explained.

Nia's face warmed with compassion. "Oh no, I hope she feels better," she said, her voice dripping with worry.

Even without Rachelle, the girls laughed, chatted, and enjoyed each other's company and the delicious treats as their voices mingled with the crackling fire. Amber took a bite of her cookie sandwich, her eyes turning to Dominique.

"Hey Dominique, these are so good! What are they?" she asked.
"They're alfajores," Dominique explained, a smile tugging at her lips. "It's a pastry from Argentina, but it's also found in other South American countries like Bolivia, Paraguay, and Peru. My mom made these. I get my Colombian side from her."

Nia's eyes shone with understanding. "So that explains the little Colombian flag on your keychain," she laughed. "I wish I could speak Spanish like you because I'm awful at it."

Dominique smiled, her eyes twinkling as she spoke, nodding with pride. "I also have my Venezuelan side from my mom, too, which is where I get my cooking skills," she continued, enthusiasm glowing on her face. "Oh, my Salvadoran and Mexican sides come from my dad."

Chapter 6

Just then, a catchy beat dropped, and Zoey's head instinctively bobbed along with the rhythm. She couldn't help it—the song was just too good. "Hey Sydney, what song is this?" she asked, tapping her fingers on the plate of her half-eaten s'more and a leftover piece of her mushroom and sausage pizza.

Sydney shrugged and pulled out her phone, her fingers quickly typing across the screen. "I don't know, let me see," she said, her face lighting up as the screen flashed. "'Independent Woman' by Destiny's Child."

"I love this song!" Nia exclaimed, leaping up from her seat. She began dancing around, her moves bursting with energy and confidence. The other girls cheered her on as she showed off her impressive hip-hop moves, her smile captivating the whole atmosphere.

When the song ended, Nia took a bow, then grinned mischievously. "That's why they voted me as the star dancer of the Midnight Prowlers!" she said proudly.

The other girls stared in shock, their jaws dropping slightly in disbelief as they watched Nia casually sit down.

"Wait, so you're the star dancer?" Zoey blurted out, her eyes grew round with shock. "No wonder that dancer from the football and basketball games was so good—those crazy moves keep her winning the captain's battles every time!"

The girls all erupted in laughter, their eyes glimmering with amusement at Nia's talent and Zoey's witty remark. They couldn't stop talking about Nia's dance moves until Sydney swiftly interrupted.

"All right, ladies, I call this game *How Well Do You Know Your Best Friends?*" she said with a grin. The girls exchanged puzzled glances at Sydney, trying to figure out what she was up to as she shuffled the cards, adding to the suspense.

"How do you play?" Hannah asked.
"It's simple," Sydney explained, finishing shuffling the cards and stacking them neatly. "One person will pull a card, read the question aloud, and answer. Then, the next person answers, too. If your answers match, you're out. The first person who has the most cards wins."

The girls nodded eagerly, their eyes illuminated with anticipation as they kicked off the game.

Dominique grabbed the first card, her fingers flipping it over as she began. *"Before living in Avalon, what city did you grow up in?"* she read aloud.

Without hesitation, Dominique looked up, her voice steady. "I'm originally from Miami," she answered. "My family and I moved to Avalon when I was three."

Nia, sitting to her right, chimed in. "I was born in Kansas City, but we moved to Avalon when I was seven," she added, her voice evoked a sense of nostalgia.

Next, it was Hannah's turn. She shifted in her spot, thinking for a second before speaking. "I've lived in Chicago since I was a baby," she said. "We moved to Avalon because my mom got a new job."

A smile pulled at the corner of Zoey's lips as she leaned forward. "I've lived in Avalon my entire life," she said, her tone bright and confident.

 Amber spoke up next, her usual soft voice rising with confidence. "I've lived in Avalon, but my parents were originally from New York," she said.

"My parents have lived in Avalon for most of their lives, right after I was born," Sydney added, calm but assured.

With everyone still in the game, Amber shuffled the deck, rapidly switching between the cards with her fingers. Then, she pulled out the next card. "Okay," she said, her eyes focusing on the question. "*After graduating high school, what do you want to major in, and what do you want to be when you grow up?*" she read.

Amber's eyes gleamed with optimism as she straightened up. "I want to major in elementary education and become a kindergarten teacher," she answered confidently.

Hannah went next, her smile beaming. "I want to major in art and become an artist. I also hope to own an art gallery someday," she said.

Zoey grinned, leaning forward. "I want to major in accounting and become a financial analyst," she said, her voice steady.

Dominique had her answer prepared, unfaltering, and coming quickly. "I want to major in chemical engineering and minor in chemistry and become a chemical engineer," she replied.

"I want to major in biochemistry and become a biochemist," Nia answered, her eyes lighting up with intensity. "Oh, and maybe an NFL cheerleader for the Chiefs, too!"

Sydney smiled, her gaze drifting as she spoke. "I want to double major in communications and public relations," she said. "I hope to become a publicist someday. I also want to play professional soccer."

The next card slid easily as Sydney pulled it from the deck. "*What do your parents do for a living?*" she read aloud, her eyes glancing around the circle.

Sydney cleared her throat before answering without hesitation. "My mom works as a nurse, and my dad works as a police detective," she said.

Hannah was quick to go next. "My mom works as an accountant, and my dad is a business coordinator," she said, smiling coyly.

Zoey followed up, her eyes bright as she leaned forward. "My mom works as a real estate agent, and my dad owns a restaurant called House of Hongdae," she said.

"Is that the restaurant in downtown Avalon?" Nia asked, her brow pressed in curiosity as she bit off her s'more, wiping the marshmallow from the left corner of her lip.

Zoey nodded with a smile. "Yep, that's the one," she replied.
"My dad usually goes there for his lunch breaks," Nia replied. "Anyway, he's the hotel manager of the Azure Isle Hotel, and my mom's a microbiologist."

Dominique was next, setting her water bottle beside her with a muffled thud. "My mom's a chemist, and my dad's a firefighter," she answered, a bold smile forming.

Amber smiled shyly, sipping her cup of fruit punch. "My mom is a dentist, and my dad is a wealth management analyst," she said.

It was now Zoey's turn. With a flick of a wrist, she pulled out a card and read it out loud: "*What's your favorite Pop-Tart flavor?*"

Zoey's eyes blinked with excitement as her face brightened. She didn't need to reconsider. "Frosted strawberry," she said, her words sharp and quick.
Dominique nodded eagerly, grinning from ear to ear. "Oh, I love frosted chocolate chip," she said.

"Frosted cookies & crème for me," Hannah blurted, her smile curving across her lips.

Nia smiled, her eyes sparkling. "Frosted s'mores are my favorite," she said.

Sydney let out a small laugh, her grin wide. "Frosted chocolate fudge is my go-to," she said, her voice light and carefree.

Amber blushed as she spoke with uncertainty. "I really love frosted raspberry," she confessed.

Zoey raised an eyebrow, a teasing grin appearing on her face. "Out of all the different flavors, why raspberry?" she snickered, her eyes gleaming with amusement and curiosity.

Amber's cheeks reddened even more, dropping her head down slightly before glancing up again. "I just really love raspberries," she admitted.

The girls giggled at Amber's cute confession, their laughter swirling around them as the fun continued. All eyes were on Hannah when she reached out for the next card. She flipped it over, her eyes scanning the words. "*What is the most tragic thing that has happened in your life?*" she said, faintly trembling.

Suddenly, the atmosphere changed. The laughter faded, replaced with a subtle tension that hung heavy in the air. The girls' eyes were fixed on Hannah, staring at the card, her fingers nervously brushing over the edges. Her mind almost went blank as she could feel her heart starting to thump. However, Hannah took a slow, steady breath, trying to calm her nerves as the gravity of the question sank in. She lifted her gaze, meeting each of her friends' eyes, before finally speaking.

"Well," she began. "When I was seven, my older sister, Caroline, disappeared, and we never found her."

The room fell silent in shock. As they felt the impact of Hannah's words, compassion spread across the girls' faces as they exchanged looks of shock and sadness. Their typical playful energy has been replaced by quiet empathy, and each face displayed a mixture of understanding and surprise.

First, Zoey spoke up, her eyes staring in disbelief. "Oh man, I'm so sorry, Hannah," she said, her voice filled with genuine sorrow. "That's awful."

Hannah nodded, a few tears escaping her cheeks as her lips trembled. "We were playing at Johnson Park back in Chicago, and Caroline and I were tossing around our favorite yellow ball," she said. "I threw it too high, and it bounced away into the woods. Caroline decided to go look for it."

Hannah's voice quivered as she continued, her words coming more slowly as she tried to process them. "She told me to watch our little sister, Sadie, and Caroline just disappeared into the woods," she said as she took a heavy breath. "At first, I didn't think much of it, but I started to get scared, so I went to look for her. Then, I heard her screaming … and calling for help. I ran back to our parents. We all rushed in to look for her but couldn't find her."

Amber's eyes bulged, her face full of disbelief. "Oh my gosh, what happened? Did the police find her?" she asked, her voice trembling with concern.

Hannah shook her head, her face clouded with sadness. "No, she was never found," she said. "We searched for days, but she was just … gone."

"Wow, that must've been horrible for you," Dominique said tenderly, her voice thick with sympathy.

The others exchanged quiet, empathic glances. Sydney felt a long pang of regret and guilt for having drawn such a difficult question from the deck. She wished she could take it back because she knew it felt heavier due to the question.

More tears streamed down Hannah's face, making it harder to hide the pain. "If I hadn't thrown the ball too high," she muttered. "She would still be here."

Nia moved closer, her arms gently wrapping around Hannah as she embraced her. They rested their heads against each other, finding solace in the quiet strength of their friendship. The group fell silent, each girl feeling the sorrow of Hannah's heartbreaking story.

"I know how you feel," Nia said softly, her voice barely above a whisper. "My twin brother, Davante, also went missing."

The other girls looked at Nia, understanding filling their expressions. "He disappeared during our freshman year," she continued. "We were about to start studying for finals, and … he just didn't come home. We still don't know what happened to him."

Tears welled up in Nia's eyes, but before she could wipe them away, Sydney and the others were there, pulling her into a reassuring, tight hug.

"I'm so sorry, Nia," Sydney murmured, her voice ringing with kindness and empathy. "That must have been really hard for you."

The group fell silent, each girl lost in her thoughts and burdened by the magnitude of Nia and Hannah's pain. After a moment, Sydney spoke up, her voice quiet but firm. "Maybe we can skip this question," she said. "It's too much … for both of you."

Hannah, wiping her tears, barely managed a grateful smile. "Thanks, guys," she said under her breath. The ache in her chest eased, comforted by the others' kindness.

 "Uh … you know," Hannah continued, clearing her throat as her voice grew lighter. "Sydney, Zoey, and I made a group chat. Do you wanna join?"

Dominique, Amber, and Nia nodded eagerly, their faces lighting up with gratitude. The relief from the heavy topic was like a breath of fresh air, lifting the gloomy cloud hanging over the group. They all exchanged phone numbers and social media handles, tapping away at their phone to add each other to each group chat. For a brief moment, the silence lingered uncomfortably, and the atmosphere remained. Finally, Hannah pulled out another card, and with a grin, the game moved forward.

"If you could be a Disney Princess, who would you be and why?" she read loudly. Hannah paused briefly, taking a deep breath as her finger tapped on the edge of the card. "I would be Belle because she's smart, independent, and loves to read," she said, her voice steady.

Sydney didn't hesitate, her eyes bright with excitement. "I'd be Jasmine because she's independent and adventurous," she said.

Zoey chimed in, leaning forward as she drank from her grape Kool-Aid. "I would choose Mulan because she's strong and brave," she said, her voice confident and steady.

Dominique nodded thoughtfully, tapping her half-empty water bottle. She paused for a moment before answering. "I'd be Ariel because I love to swim, and she's curious and determined to explore the world beyond," she said.

"I would pick Cinderella because she's kind and always stays true to herself," Amber said, her voice soft and steady. "No matter what."

Nia thought for a moment, her gaze drifting as she considered. "I'd be Princess Tiana because she's hardworking and determined to achieve her dreams," she answered.

A remarkable and unspoken bond grew as the game progressed. Despite their differences, interests, and personalities, they all had similar qualities and values that brought them closer: kindness, strength, and a quiet sense of determination.

Amber turned to Hannah, an inquisitive, playful grin pulled at the corners of her lips. "Hey Hannah, if Caroline were here right now, what Disney Princess would she be?" she asked, her voice serene and filled with warmth and curiosity.

Hannah's subdued smile returned, her eyes distant as she thought about Caroline. "Well, she would've been Princess Aurora," she said, her voice low but confident. "She's always kind, gentle and has a beautiful spirit…just like her."

The girls all nodded quietly, their smiles and faces reflecting understanding. A new, peaceful, positive energy filled the void between them, strengthening their bond.

"Hey guys, why don't we call it a night?" Sydney suggested with a yawn. The girls agreed, ready for some rest after a fun night. They gathered their snack plates, tossing them and leftover crumbs into the trash before heading inside. Sleeping bags were spread across the living room floor, forming a circle where they all gathered. Laughter and chatter filled the air as they settled in, their bond stronger than ever. As they drifted off to sleep, the enveloping feeling of their new friendships wrapped around them like a cozy blanket. They had started as strangers, but through their matching necklaces and the moments they'd shared, it blossomed into something more profound—something that would always last.

The next morning, car engines pulling outside cut through the house's tranquil humming. Dominique and Nia's parents arrived first to pick them up. Following a round of hugs and goodbyes, it was time for Hannah to go. Maggie was talking to Sydney's parents, who were busy in the kitchen making breakfast. Mrs. Barnes, in teal scrubs and comfortable white tennis shoes, had her dark brown hair pulled back neatly in a ponytail. Her light skin glowed in the hazy morning light, and when she saw Sydney and Hannah, her striking brown eyes lit up with a welcoming smile. Mr. Barnes followed, his smooth bald head shining in the sunlight. His warm brown skin and kind brown eyes gave him a friendly, approachable presence. He slipped off his black leather jacket, revealing a royal blue long-sleeved shirt. A police badge hung from a chain around his neck. After saying his goodbyes, he headed to the kitchen, ready to make himself a cup of coffee.

Maggie turned to Mrs. Barnes with a bright smile, her voice light. "I hope Hannah wasn't too much trouble last night, Jennifer," she said with a hushed laugh.

Jennifer shook her head, offering a reassuring smile. "Not at all, Maggie," she replied cheerfully. "Sydney told me that Hannah's a sweetheart."

"It's nice to see Sydney making new friends outside of the soccer team," Mr. Barnes said, joining in on their conversation.

Zoey and Amber said their goodbyes and stepped outside, where their parents waited. Hannah watched them go, a bittersweet smile forming across her lips as she waved them off. She and Sydney followed suit, making their way toward the kitchen.

"I'll see you at school tomorrow?" asked Sydney.
Hannah nodded, her smile still lingering. "Yeah," she said reflectively. Before their conversation could continue, Maggie's voice cut through the moment. She stood in the doorway, a faint smile on her face, her head tilting slightly as her eyes met Hannah's. "Ready to go?" she asked, her voice caring and inviting.

 Hannah grinned, the ache of the moment fading. "Yeah," she said, her tone brighter. She turned to Sydney's parents, her pleasant smile widening. "It was nice to meet you, Mr. and Mrs. Barnes."

Sydney's parents both smiled brightly, their expressions gracious and genuine. "Likewise, Hannah," said Mrs. Barnes, her voice kind and welcoming. "We'll see you around."

"Feel free to come visit anytime," said Mr. Barnes.

As they stepped out of the house and climbed into the car, the effect of the fun night lingered in Hannah's heart. With another smile pulling at her lips, she leaned back in her seat. She was overcome with gratitude for her new friends, their shared memories, and laughter. The buzz of her phone cut through the peaceful drive. She pulled it from her lap and unlocked the screen, her heart beating fast as her eyes scanned the message. Nia had just sent a photo of them together—herself, Zoey, Sydney, Dominique, Hannah, and Amber—smiling and huddled in the living room.

"Thank you for the amazing night," the text read.
Hannah gazed at the photo and felt a wave of positivity and contentment wash over her. There they were, all smiles, capturing something she knew they would never forget. She felt the bond between them, so strong and genuine. Smiling, she tapped "like" on the picture and noticed everyone else followed suit. Something special happened that night—something they would never forget.

As they rolled past a café, Maggie turned to her with a grin. "I found a bakery ten minutes away from here," she said, her eyes sparkling with exhilaration. "How about a breakfast brioche sandwich?"

Before she could respond, Hannah's stomach growled loudly, making her laugh. "Yes, please!" she eagerly replied.

On Monday morning, Hannah was going to her first-period class, slipping her AirPods and phone into her gray-blue jean jacket. She rounded a corner when a voice called out to her.

"*Hannah!*" someone shrieked in full fury.
She turned around and saw Heather storming toward her, an aura of anger rushing her like a storm cloud.

She groaned under her breath, her frustration building up inside her. She had no interest in facing her again, especially after what happened in chemistry class. Ignoring her, she quickened the pace, hoping Heather would take the hint. But as soon as she rounded another corner, to her dismay, her path was suddenly blocked by Carleigh, Molly, and Kaliyah. Hannah sighed, exasperated, as she faced them, already bracing for the confrontation.

"Can you guys move? I'm already late for class," she said, trying to keep her cool.

The girls just smirked, not moving an inch. It was almost like they were enjoying every second of making Hannah squirm. Heather stepped forward, a sly grin spreading across her face.

"You know, you really made a fool out of me in chemistry class on Friday," she said. "I can't believe you would do that to me, especially in front of my mom."

Hannah rolled her eyes, shaking her head as if she couldn't believe they were still talking about it. "Heather, I didn't do anything," she said, her voice growing firmer. "You made a fool out of yourself."

"Oh, please. You're just jealous because you can't keep up with the classy stereotypes of Avalon High," Heather said, a smug smile forming. "You will always be the classless Chicago outsider. Nothing will ever change that."

Hannah had had enough. The anger bubbled up inside her, and her patience was wearing thin. She was tired of being pushed around by Heather and her friends. In a split second, her demeanor completely changed. If someone keeps pushing her buttons, she never backs down in any situation. She always stands her ground. She would clench her fists and narrow her eyes before someone could finish speaking. Every time she spoke up, her voice quickly cut through conversations, interrupting anyone who would cross her.

"You know something, Heather, I don't have to fit into your so-called classy stereotype," she said. "In fact, I think it's pathetic that you have to put others down to make yourself look better."

Heather's smug smirk dropped, her jaw slightly hitting the floor as her eyes gaped in surprise. As Hannah turned to leave, Heather tightly gripped her hair. However, instead of flinching, Hannah reacted swiftly, pushing Heather back just enough to make her almost stumble.

"I'm done, Heather! I'm not gonna deal with your antics anymore because you don't scare me," she said, her gaze unwavering. "You're the one with no class. You're pathetic."

Heather and her friends were frozen, taken aback by Hannah's sudden change in demeanor. They had never seen this side of her before. Hannah's words echoed in the hallway, loud enough for everyone to hear. Her voice reverberated as she passed each student until she reached Sydney, who witnessed the whole thing, her eyes locked in disbelief.

"Hey, what happened?" asked Sydney. "You okay?"
Hannah quickly told Sydney what had happened with Heather, and Sydney's eyes flashed in fury. Just then, Heather charged toward them, her steps heavy and meticulous. Hannah was caught off guard and didn't even see her coming. Before she could act, Sydney jumped in front of Hannah without thinking, blocking Heather's way. She glared at Heather, daring her to take another step.

Heather sneered, her eyes blazing with rage. "Move out of the way, Barnes," she demanded.

"Make me," Sydney said, her voice in a low growl.
Each of their words lashed out, their voices drawing the attention of more students around them. They watched with wide-eyed astonishment as the tension crackled in the air. Heather got right up in Sydney's face, their eyes staring directly at each other. However, Sydney didn't flinch. Instead, she held her ground, stepping forward with her chin lifted defiantly. Still,

Heather didn't back down. She lunged forward again, but before she could get any closer, Zoey stepped in, pushing Heather away with surprising strength.

"Get out of my face!" Sydney yelled.
Hannah, Sydney, and Zoey stood their ground, not moving an inch as they stared into Heather's glaring eyes, their standoff far from over. With Carleigh, Kaliyah, and Molly by Heather's side, the shouting match between them grew louder and louder, drawing more attention from more students and even the teachers into the scene. Nia and Amber appeared, their ears ringing through the commotion. As soon as Nia heard the heated words from the girls, her eyes flashed with boldness and no hesitation. She stepped into the chaos without a word, letting her backpack drop to the floor with a thud.

"Hey! Back off, Barringer!" Nia shouted, her voice fierce and strong.
 Nia's words flew fast, each thicker than the last, as she took Heather head-on, defending Hannah, Sydney, and Zoey with a fierce energy that left no room for doubt. It was clear Nia was not afraid to speak up, her fiery side shining through as she made it known that she wasn't backing down.

As the shouting match continued, the teachers finally stepped in, breaking up the chaos and ordering everyone to go to class. Even then, Heather didn't stop. She kept ranting, her face now flashing bright red. She couldn't get to Hannah, Sydney, Zoey, and Nia, thanks to a male Hispanic teacher who stood in her way, gently holding her back to prevent the situation from escalating. Amber stepped in, trying to calm Nia down, but Nia's frustration continued to simmer beneath the surface. When Heather spoke again, her voice still sharp, it only fueled Nia's anger further.

"So what, girl? You don't run this school," she shouted, her fiery eyes still glaring. "Get over yourself!"

Zoey couldn't help but clap in amusement, a smirk spreading across her face while Nia screamed, "Bye!" as Heather and her friends stormed off, their heads hung in defeat.

Sydney noticed Nia breathing heavily as her shoulders tensed up, barely containing frustration. Without a word, she stepped closer, gently grasping Nia's wrist. "She's not worth it, Nia," she said, her voice soothing. "Just take a breath."

Slowly, Nia's shoulders relaxed as she took a deep breath, realizing she had let her emotions get the best of her. They, along with Hannah, Zoey, and Amber, all checked in with each other, making sure everyone was okay. After a few moments, they exchanged knowing smiles and went their separate ways, promising to see each other again in class.

By the time the bell rang, signaling the end of their fourth-period class, Hannah, Sydney, and Zoey exchanged eager looks, their pace quickening as they headed to homeroom. They walked side by side, their laughter and conversations echoing through the hallways until they reached the classroom.

Hannah and Sydney headed straight for the first double desk in the third row while Zoey chose the desk next to theirs. Just as they were settling in, Amber walked through the door. Her eyes twinkled when she saw them, beaming with thrill. In response, Hannah, Sydney, and Zoey grinned, their enthusiasm matching Amber's.

"Hi, friends! How are you guys?" she exclaimed, making her way to sit beside Zoey.

One by one, the rest of the class poured in, finding their seats with a combination of chatter and shuffling feet. However, Mrs. Farrow was nowhere in sight. With the final students settling in and sliding into their desks, the clatter of voices grew louder. Hannah glanced around, her eyes landing on her friends. She could feel her heart beat a little faster. This was her chance to thank her friends for having her back earlier and standing by her side.

"I never got the chance to thank you guys," she said with a sincere smile. "I told you, I've got your back. Actually, *we've* got your back," Sydney replied with a grin, her voice filled with caring and reassurance.

Zoey grinned, her eyes sparkling with mischief. "Girls stick up for each other," she said. "We showed Heather that we wouldn't tolerate her shenanigans." She gave a wink, a confident smile forming across her lips.

The four of them burst into laughter, echoing through the room. Their bright, broad smiles were more expressive than words could ever be. They leaned into one another, their laughter slowly fading, each laugh making them feel lighter. With every moment spent together, they grew a little stronger and a little closer. The world didn't seem so heavy anymore. Even Zoey's joke had them laughing harder, the joy between them making everything else feel small.

Suddenly, the atmosphere in the room shifted as Heather, Carleigh, Molly, and Kaliyah walked in, drawing everyone's attention. The four girls locked eyes on Hannah, Sydney, Zoey, and Amber, their eyes sharp and unwavering. Heather and Carleigh moved to the front of the room, choosing the double desk directly across from Hannah and Sydney. The seats were far from Zoey and Amber, and neither side made a move to show recognition. Molly and Kaliyah slid into the desk behind them. Without a word, they pulled out bottles of nail polish. The sharp click of the caps echoed in the quietness. They painted their nails, their actions nonchalant and deliberate as if the rest of the class didn't exist. The chill of their silence hung in the air, leaving everyone else feeling the divide.

Amber leaned in toward the girls, her voice barely a whisper. "I can't believe they're in our homeroom," she muttered.

The tension in the room was getting thicker, almost like hearing a pin drop. Then, a girl with pale skin, strawberry blonde hair in wild curls, and piercing emerald green eyes stood up. She wore a yellow crewneck short-sleeved shirt layered with lace chiffon, black leggings, and brown wedge sandals. As she turned to face the class, an optimistic smile flashed across her face, breaking the heavy silence and easing the tension in the room.

"Excuse me, everyone," she said, her voice carrying above the buzz of the classroom. "As your reigning school president, I have an important announcement to make." She paused for effect, clearing her throat before continuing. "As we are currently planning this year's upcoming dance, we will be sharing the events and activities leading up to it."

Before she could continue, Dominique and Nia walked in, causing another stir of liveliness from Hannah, Sydney, Zoey, and Amber. The two of them made their way to the double desk directly across from Amber and Zoey, settling in casually.

"Sorry, we're late," Nia said, grinning sheepishly.

Chapter 7

Heather and her friends immediately stiffened. The atmosphere grew heavier once again. Unspoken words filled the air. Heather, Carleigh, Kaliyah, and Molly exchanged uneasy glares, their eyes drifting toward Dominique and Nia. The tension was palpable, making it impossible to ignore. Their silent scowls spoke volumes, with their faces fixed in tight frowns. The room fell into an even starker silence. Everyone waited for someone to say something—until Nia broke the stillness.

"Obviously, Mrs. Farrow isn't here yet," Nia continued, her voice cutting through the tension. "But…I'm in the mood for a shopping spree today."

She glanced at Hannah, Sydney, and Zoey, giving them a brief, almost unnoticed look. It was her way of checking in and ensuring they were still okay from the shouting match.

"Hannah, Sydney, Zoey, you game?" she asked, her voice tight with a hint of desperation.

Hannah shook her head with a small, nervous chuckle. "No, I'm good," she said.

The tension hung like a dense fog that no one else wanted to walk through as the room fell into a more intense silence. No one knew what to say after everything that had just gone down in the hallway until Dominique finally spoke up next.

"Actually, right now, Heather, do you mind if I say something real quick?" she asked, her voice calm but firm.

Heather scoffed, rolling her eyes at Dominique, but after a moment, she shrugged as she set aside the bottle of gold nail polish.

"Fine," she muttered. "Say what you want."

Dominique inhaled deeply. "Look, I heard some things that's been happening between you guys," she said, her voice still firm. "I just need to make something clear. After what went down, we need to establish some boundaries. So…I can't let you *EVER* talk to any of us like that again."

Heather's eyes narrowed into a fierce glare, her anger boiling at being called out. Everyone held their breath, hoping something would break the tension, but it was no use. Dominique's words hung high, blunt yet critical, like a challenge no one could ignore.

"From now on, we can go our separate ways, do whatever you want," Dominique continued. "But … if you need to say something to any of us, you can go through me. Like girl to girl. I just wanna establish that—"

Heather scoffed again, loud enough to cut off Dominique mid-sentence. She opened her mouth to respond, but before she could, the class president jumped into the conversation, her voice slicing through the growing tension.

"Um … can I say something?" she asked, standing up. "Dominique, I appreciate you defending everyone and speaking up, but let me explain." She paused, clearing her throat before continuing. "Before you guys got here, Heather and her friends did nothing when they walked in. So, I don't want you two to create any animosity between each other, and I think we should forget that this happened and—"

 Heather's face flashed with shock and anger as her eyes shot open. Before the class president could finish, she cut her off mid-sentence, her voice rising with frustration. "Hang on, Lola! What are you trying to say, Guerra?" she demanded.

Before Dominique could respond, Nia spoke up, her voice dripping with sarcasm. "I've heard of mean girls before, but this is ridiculous," she laughed dismissively, tossing a strand of her hair back.

Dominique could feel Heather's vibe and need to be the center of attention. Every word and action was aimed at making herself look perfect. She felt a surge of frustration bubbling up, but she maintained her composure. "You're quite full of yourself," she called out.

"How dare you?!" Heather yelled, standing up from her seat, her fists clenched. "I am *so* not full of myself!"

Dominique stood tall, not backing down. "You are out of line. You always think it's about you," she said.

Heather's jaw tightened even more as she lunged toward Dominique, her eyes burning with fury. Before she could get close, Hannah jumped to her feet, stepping between them like a shield. Forcefully, she pushed Heather, her eyes flaming, daring Heather to take another step. Heather froze from the chill of warning in Hannah's stare. Dominique didn't move, still keeping her cool, though her voice was sharp when she spoke again.

"What are you doing?" she asked, her gaze still fixed on Heather.
Just then, Mrs. Farrow walked into the room. Her eyebrows shot up, and her piercing blue eyes blazed in surprise. The air seemed to tighten as her expression sharpened before anyone could blink. With unexpected quickness, she stepped between Hannah and Heather and firmly but gently pulled them apart. Her light honey-brown hair tumbled over her shoulders, sleek against the intensity of her gaze as she glanced from one girl to the other.

"All right, everyone, calm down!" she said sternly. "Now, what is going on here?"

None of them said a word. Everyone watched as the girls resumed their bickering, their voices rising again, as the room fell into an eerie silence. Before things could go any further, Mrs. Farrow intervened again, instantly silencing everyone. She was not the teacher who often took sides, but right now, there was no mistaking that her presence meant things were about to change.

"I don't care who started it," she said, concentrating on Heather. "Heather, you're going to have to apologize."

Heather shot a sharp look at the others, rolling her eyes. With a heavy sigh, she mumbled an apology under her breath. Finally, everyone slowly returned to their seats as the suspense in the room died down. Again, she glared intensely at the girls as she sank into her chair. They were quick to return the look, their eyes sharp and unyielding.

After homeroom, Hannah, Sydney, Zoey, Dominique, Amber, and Nia headed to the cafeteria, still chatting excitedly about the confrontation with Heather, Carleigh, Molly, and Kaliyah.

"You should've seen Hannah!" Sydney exclaimed, practically bouncing with elation as she walked beside Dominique. "She totally put Heather in her place."

Hannah shrugged nonchalantly, a tiny grin forming at the corner of her lips. "Oh, shucks, it's no problem," she replied.

Nia jumped in, her voice full of energy. "Not as awesome as Dominique calling out Heather in homeroom," she said, flickering a grin. "I was like, *yes!* She showed Heather she's not playing any games."

Zoey glanced at the girls as they turned a corner. "You know, I'm glad I met all of you. You guys are the coolest," she said.

The girls exchanged smiles, an unspoken sense of victory in the air. They all knew that standing up to Heather and her friends had somehow made them closer than ever. However, Amber trailed behind them, her feet shuffling slower with each step. Her head hung low, her eyes gazing at the floor, while her stomach let out a loud, hungry growl.

"I don't feel like going to the cafeteria," she admitted unenthusiastically. Zoey caught Amber's lack of enthusiasm and gave a quick nod. "Yeah, I don't want to eat the meatloaf anyway," she said, her tone marked with sarcasm as she shot a knowing glance at Amber.

With a cheeky grin, Dominique's eyes lit up as an idea popped into her head. "What if we skip the cafeteria and head to the Grilled Cheese Gallery instead?" she asked.

Hannah raised an eyebrow, intrigued. "The Grilled Cheese Gallery? What's that?" she asked, her curiosity piqued.

"It's a grilled cheese place, just twenty minutes off campus," Dominique explained. "Trust me, it's worth it."

Amber hesitated, her voice meek with uncertainty. "Wait, what about fifth period?" she asked, sounding a little unsure.

Dominique brushed a strand of hair behind her ear, her grin confident and determined. "Don't worry, we'll be back before fifth period," she said reassuringly. "Besides, we're allowed to go off campus for lunch. Not to mention, my mood today is basically screaming for some off-campus food."

Nia's and Zoey's faces ignited, their liveliness impossible to miss. Even Amber, her initial reluctance fading, couldn't help but perk up at the thought of skipping the cafeteria. Sydney and Hannah shared a mutual, knowing glance before nodding in agreement as they passed the cafeteria doors. The group made their way to the parking lot, and Dominique slid her hand into the small pocket of her laptop backpack, pulling out her car keys. Her eyes lit up with a grin of satisfaction and joy. Just then, the distinct sound of a car horn echoed through the lot. A royal blue Acura MDX rolled into view, its headlights glowing faintly in broad daylight.

Zoey's eyes widened, and her jaw dropped in shock. "Wait, that's *your* car?" she asked, her voice full of disbelief.
Dominique grinned, clearly proud. "Yep. Got it after summer break," she chuckled, her voice filled with pride. "And it's the newest model."

The girls eagerly rushed to the car, pulling the doors open. Inside, the soft, parchment-colored seats seemed to shine in the sunlight. Nia, Amber, Hannah, and Zoey piled into the backseat, their laughter echoing as they settled in. Sydney hopped into the passenger seat, her eyes sparkling with pleasure. Dominique slid into the driver's seat, brushing the smooth leather as she started the engine. The car hummed to life with a purring roar, the cool air rushing as they all settled in, preparing to drive off. The low purr of the engine persisted in the atmosphere.

As they drove away, Dominique steered the car down a narrow road. The air grew foggier and colder as the trees on both sides grew thicker, casting dark shadows across the windshield. An uncomfortable tension descended upon the girls as the winding path led them deeper into the forest.

Sydney glanced at Dominique with a raised eyebrow, a tiny spark of doubt in her gaze. "Uh … are you sure we should be taking this route?" she asked.

Dominique kept her hands steady on the wheel, her eyes locked in focus intently on the road, unfazed by the dense woods surrounding them.

"Yeah, it'll take us to the Grilled Cheese Gallery," she replied, her voice shaking with hesitant confidence. "Like I said, just about twenty minutes away."

As they continued down the road, the air grew thicker. Then, without warning, a trail of dark smoke appeared out of nowhere, swirling across the road in front of them. Dominique pursed her brows, struggling to concentrate, but the smoke condensed rapidly, blocking her vision entirely. Through the haze, a silhouette emerged in the mist—a woman standing motionless in the middle of the road. Her form was barely visible, swallowed by the fog. Dominique's heart slammed against her chest. She gasped loudly, gripping the wheel tightly, swerving violently to the side to avoid the woman. Her eyes expanded in terror.

"Watch out!" Nia screamed.
The tires screeched against the pavement, leaving numerous dark skid marks. Panicked screams filled the car as they struggled to brace for impact. Before Dominique could regain control, the car slid down a steep hill, plunging into the woods. Finally, the car came to a complete stop with a heavy thud. The girls staggered out, shaken but miraculously unharmed, stumbling over each other. Dominique turned toward them, her face pale and eyes wide with worry.

"Is everyone okay?" she asked, her voice still shaky.
Hannah nodded, inhaling briskly. "I'm fine, just a little shaken up," she replied.

Amber's hands trembled as she glanced back at the wreckage. "I've never felt like this before," she whispered, her voice still in a daze.

Her head rocking from the crash and her vision still blurred, Sydney turned to Dominique. "Next time, Dom, take my advice and take the other shortcut," she said.

The girls groaned in unison as they surveyed the damage. Dominique's car had crashed into a tree, one of its headlights was shattered, glass shards spread across the ground, and the front end was completely damaged.

Dominique crouched down, her face dramatically falling. "Oh no, my car!" she whined, her voice exaggerated.

 Hannah placed a hand on her shoulder, trying to comfort her. "It's not that bad, Dominique," she said.

"Yeah, you'll be fine," said Sydney, her tone more consoling and uplifting. Still visibly shaken, Amber placed her hand on her head, her gaze gradually drifting away. "I don't know, guys. It looks pretty bad to me," she said, her voice quavering with uneasiness.

Sydney shot a sharp look at Amber, scoffing at her remark, brushing her words aside.

Nia rubbed her neck, wincing as she glanced around the woods. "What *was* that?" she asked. "I mean … what just happened?"
Dominique slightly opened her jaw, struggling to come up with the words. "I … I don't know," she explained, still baffled. "It looked like a woman in the middle of the road."

Zoey, still disoriented, rolled her eyes. "Oh, come on," she shrugged, trying to lighten the mood. "It was probably a deer or something."

Dominique quickly got up, her face exuding frustration. "I'm telling you, it was a woman in the middle of the road," she insisted. "I saw her with my own eyes!"

Amber fumbled with her phone, desperately searching for a signal. However, after a few failed attempts, her eyes darted around, and she panted frantically. "Guys, I can't get any signal out here," she said, trembling. "What are we gonna do?"

Nia pulled out her phone and stared at the blank screen. "Yeah, I can't get anything either," she said.

Hannah glanced around, thinking fast. "Let's split up and see if we can look for a signal," she said, her voice steady despite the tension. "We need to call for help."

The girls scattered, each trying desperately to get a connection. A few hours later, Nia, Dominique, and Zoey regrouped at the spot where they had split up, disappointed and empty-handed.

Dominique paced back and forth, her hands fidgeting. "I'm going to be so late," she whimpered, her voice cracking with panic. "Mrs. Glasgow is going to kill me."

Zoey crossed her arms, her patience wearing thin. "Well, maybe if you had listened to Sydney, we wouldn't be in this mess," she snapped.

Dominique's face turned bright red. She stepped right up to Zoey, her fists clenched. "Oh, so now it's my fault?!" she shouted, her words cutting through the air.

Zoey's retort was equally heated. With each word, the two girls' voices grew louder as they yelled over one another. Nia hurried over and stood between them.

"Hey! Stop!" she yelled, her hands grabbing both of their shoulders. Neither girl moved for a moment. The tension in the air was ominous, but the shouting stopped. They all breathed slowly. At that moment, Sydney and Hannah returned, their faces etched with concern and defeat.

Nia glanced at them, panting. "Anything?" she asked.
Hannah shook her head, letting out a frustrated sigh. "No, nothing," Hannah replied, her shoulders slumping.

The girls stood there for a moment, catching their breath. Then, Dominique's brow wrinkled unexpectedly as a sudden realization struck her. "Wait … Where's Amber?" she asked, her voice wavering with confusion.

The girls looked at each other, puzzled, their eyes scanning around the forest. Amber was nowhere in sight. Before anyone could speak, a voice called from deep within the forest. "Hey guys, I think I got something!" Amber's voice called out, clear but distant.

The girls didn't hesitate. Their feet pounding on the forest floor, they rushed toward Amber's voice. The closer they got, the faster they ran, but something didn't feel right. Amber's voice remained at the same distance regardless of how fast they moved. She was coming toward them, but she appeared not to be moving. She seemed … frozen.

"Amber, wait!" a confused Hannah called out.
But Amber didn't seem to hear her. She kept walking as if she didn't even notice. Then, without warning, she stepped right into something—an invisible, shimmering wall. The girls stopped in their tracks, staring in disbelief, unsure of what they had just seen.

"What just happened?" Zoey uttered, her trembling voice intertwining with awe and worry.

"I-I don't know," Sydney stuttered. "Should we follow her?"
Before anyone could answer, they all stepped forward, following Amber as they passed through the invisible wall. Then, the world around them changed. The air shimmered, and the forest seemed to transform. It appeared to be empty, but it was far from it. Above them, towering trees glistened in the gentle sunlight, their leaves sparkling like jewels. Waterfalls cascaded down rocky cliffs, sending mist into the air. The tranquility was broken only by the soft ripple of streams as they passed through the lush trees, bushes, and shrubs. The sweet fragrance of flowers filled the air, and warm rays of sunlight bathed it in a soft, golden glow. Small villages peeked through the trees in the distance, their houses crafted from stone, twigs, and leaves. The girls stood in stunned silence, taking in the beauty

and mystery of the strange new world around them.

"Wow, this place … is incredible," Sydney whispered, her eyes awestruck as she stared at the vibrant flowers and sparkling water.

"I've never seen anything like it, Nia added.
"It looks like a different version of the forest," Dominique said, her voice full of wonder and fascination. "It's almost like … like … "

"Magic?" Amber finished, her eyes meeting Dominique's and Nia's with curiosity.

The girls wandered through the trees, their footsteps barely making a sound on the soft, mossy ground. It seemed like the entire world had paused, and everything was quiet and serene. After countless hours of wandering, Hannah shook her head, her thoughts snapping back to reality. "Okay, guys. We need to find a spot with a signal," she said.

They nodded in agreement, then split up, each heading in different directions. Minutes turned to hours, but nothing changed. They scanned the sky, the rocks, and the trees for any sign, but the silence dragged on. Zoey continued to search the area, her eyes darting quickly between the shadows and the trees. Suddenly, her feet froze, stopping her in her tracks. She squinted, leaning forward, trying to make sense of what she was seeing. There, partially hidden by vines and moss, was a dark, narrow hole nestled between two large boulders. It looked like a hidden tunnel.

"Hey guys, check this out!" she called, gesturing behind a tangle of shrubs. The girls exchanged curious glances before rushing over to where Zoey had disappeared. They reached the entrance to the hidden tunnel and followed her into the bushes. Their footsteps reverberated in the darkness as they entered after a brief moment of hesitation. The tunnel opened into a vast cavern, its walls lit by dozens of hazy, glowing lights. At the center of the cavern stood a majestic tree, its trunk old and sturdy. Surrounding it was a magical circle made up of twelve vibrant gemstones: diamond, emerald, alexandrite, ruby, peridot, sapphire, pink tourmaline, yellow citrine, orange topaz, garnet, amethyst, and aquamarine. Each stone pulsed with its energy, creating a charge of magic that seemed to vibrate through the air.

"Whoa!" Hannah said.
"This is … amazing," Dominique murmured, her eyes alert as she took in the sight before her.

The girls stepped forward slowly, standing in the glowing circle. A strange energy pulsed from the gemstones, filling the air with a rich, harmonic vibration. Each girl moved slowly and quietly, their thoughts lost in the mystery. Then, Hannah's phone buzzed in her jeans pocket amid the silence. Her shoulders jumped slightly, startled by the sound. She pulled it out and glanced at the screen. Her phone now had four full bars of signal. She held it up high, her face a mixture of triumph and intense focus.

"Yes!" she exclaimed. "Okay, I got something!"
The girls turned toward her, watching eagerly as Hannah dialed her parents, her fingers moving swiftly over the screen. Suddenly, Nia's attention shifted to Zoey's necklace. A bright, flashing purple light beamed from it, almost like it was coming to life.

"Hey Zoey, what's up with your necklace?" she asked, her curiosity piqued.

Zoey blinked, her face written with confusion before her gaze dropped to her necklace. "What are you talking about?" she asked.

Then, her eyes widened in shock as the glow caught her attention again. "Wait! Why is my necklace glowing?" she gasped, her voice rising with panic.

Sydney darted to her necklace. The bright, vivid orange light seemed to vibrate with life on its own, mirroring Zoey's. "Mine's glowing, too!" she exclaimed.

One by one, the girls glanced at their necklaces. Slowly, the gemstones began to glow, each one flickering to life. At first, the light was dim, barely a shimmer, but then it rapidly grew brighter, pulsing with intense energy. As if drawn by an unseen force, each girl felt a sudden tug, pulling her toward the gemstone that matched her birthstone. It was as if the gems were calling out to them.

Hannah's feet moved toward the emerald, Sydney felt herself pulled to the topaz, Zoey drifted to the amethyst, Dominique to the sapphire, Amber toward the aquamarine, and Nia to the tourmaline. They stood motionless, struggling to understand what was happening, their eyes locked on the glowing gems. The light grew even brighter, engulfing them in a radiant glow. The gemstones vibrated with power as the girls felt a surge of energy coursing through them.

Suddenly, their eyes began to glow—green for Hannah, orange for Sydney, purple for Zoey, blue for Dominique, turquoise for Amber, and pink for Nia. Without warning, the light from their necklaces and the gems flickered, and the whir subsided into silence. The girls looked at each other, speechless, their hearts still pounding in their chests. Then, the ground trembled beneath them out of the blue, and the air vibrated with a low rumble.

Amber's voice broke the silence. "What was that?" she pondered, her voice trembling with uncertainty.

Nia shook her head, her face turning pale. "I don't want to know, and I don't wanna find out," she replied.

Hannah's mind was racing, searching for a way out. She looked around the cavern, the strange energy still reverberating in the air. Her eyes landed on the tunnel—the same one they had used to enter the cavern. "Come on," she yelled firmly, taking charge. "This way!"

Without another word, the girls followed her, the gentle radiance of the circle fading behind them as they hurried through the cavern. The world around them seemed strangely still, as if time was slowing down. Soon, they reached the same invisible wall they had encountered earlier, its glistening surface barely visible in the low light.

Sydney hesitated, her brow crimping. "Are you sure about this?" she asked.

Hannah did not hesitate. She gestured toward the shimmering invisible wall, her hand steady despite the uncertainty around them. "This is our way out," she yelled, her voice full of determination.

The girls exchanged uncertain looks but trusted Hannah without question. Together, they stepped forward, crossing the invisible barrier. The surrounding air rippled around them as they passed through, and in an instant, the forest disappeared. They were back in their world, standing in the fading light of the sunset. The magnitude of their strange experience settled in like a thick fog. Just as the girls took a collective breath, trying to calm their racing hearts, a sharp voice rang out from behind them, jolting them all upright.

"Hey! What are you girls doing here?" the voice demanded.
They whirled around to see a park ranger standing behind them, her expression serious, and one hand placed firmly on her hip.

Hannah stepped forward, her heart still pounding in her chest, and tried to keep her composure as her eyes locked on the ranger. "We are so sorry," she explained, her voice full of sincerity. "We were just on our way to the Grilled Cheese Gallery when we got into an accident. We were trying to call our parents."

The park ranger's intensity relaxed to some extent as she listened, but her expression stayed firm. After a moment, she let out a reassuring sigh. "Well, you're in luck that I found you," she said. "All right, I'll help you out, but I do not want to see any of you back here. This part of the forest has been restricted for years. Understood?"

The girls nodded quickly, their thanks tumbling in a rush. The ranger smiled kindly and offered to call a mechanic to fix Dominique's car. A huge wave of relief flooded the girls as they exchanged looks of unspoken gratitude. After everything that had happened, they were so glad they wouldn't have to walk back home. As they waited, Hannah pulled the others close, her voice dropping to a near whisper.

"From now on, we can't tell anyone about the forest," she said quietly but sternly. "Not ever!" Her words became more serious as she looked them directly in the eyes.

The girls nodded, their heads moving in unison as the cloud of the secret hung heavily around them like a large cloak. It seemed as though the silence was closing in on them. Before long, Dominique's car sputtered to life. Instead of heading to the Grilled Cheese Gallery, they turned toward home. They dropped Hannah off first, waving goodbye with promises to see each other the next day. Hannah stepped through the door of her house. Her mind was still spinning from everything that had happened. The magic forest, the magic circle … It all felt so familiar, as if she had dreamed of these things before, but she couldn't put her finger on it. She was lost in thought when her mom's voice cut through the haze.

"Hannah! Oh, thank God you're all right," Maggie exclaimed, her voice filled with worry.

Jeremy, standing beside her, let out a sharp gasp, his face almost turning pale. "Oh my God, what happened?" he asked.

Her parents rushed before Hannah could say anything, pulling her into a tight hug. Their eyes scanned her, searching for any sign of injury. "We were so worried about you!" Maggie scolded, tears threatened to fall from her eyes. "Why didn't you call us?"

Hannah let out a heavy sigh, a knot of guilt forming in her stomach. She knew she should tell her parents what had really happened, but she had promised her friends that she wouldn't say a word about the invisible wall, the magic forest, or the magic circle. They wouldn't believe her anyway. She didn't want them to think she was crazy.

"I'm sorry. I didn't want to worry you guys," she said. "I had a little accident. I tried calling you, but I didn't have service. I'm okay now. The problem's been taken care of."

Her parents hugged her tighter, relief pouring over their faces. "We're just so glad you're safe," Jeremy scolded gently. "Next time, just call us if you're going to be out late or something."

Hannah nodded, the guilt still gnawing at her. Her heart ached as she saw the worry in their eyes. But beneath it all, she knew she had made the right decision by keeping the secret.

Later, after dinner, Hannah changed into her pajamas and noiselessly crept toward her parents' room. The soft murmur of their breathing told her they were already asleep. She could hear Sadie's faint snoring from her room. Hannah tiptoed back to her room, the weight of exhaustion settling in her mind. Just as she was about to collapse into bed, her phone buzzed with a text message from the group chat.

Sydney's text message popped up first: *"What did your parents say?"* Dominique's message followed right after. *"Thanks to that woman who stood in the middle of the road, my mom grounded me for FOUR MONTHS! Now my car's gonna be in the shop for two weeks."*

Nia's message appeared next. *"I hate lying to my parents. I don't know how long*

I can keep doing it."

Amber added, "*Same here. I had to make up a story. My parents are WAY too overprotective.*"

Hannah took a deep breath, her fingers hovering over her phone. She typed: "*It's okay. I told my parents we had a car accident.*"

Zoey responded promptly, "*At least I didn't mention the magic forest.*"
Hannah quickly typed her response. "*Remember, no one can know what we saw. It's our secret.*"

A flood of thumbs-up emojis filled the screen, and Hannah finally felt at ease for the first time since this whole thing began. Setting her phone aside, she buried herself into her pillow, hoping its softness would block out the odd things that had happened that day. Yet, as she closed her eyes, questions continued to race through her head.

Why were she and her friends the only ones who could see the invisible wall that led to the magic forest? How could they see the glowing circle with twelve different gemstones, including theirs? And most importantly, how was her necklace connected to the circle when it started to glow?

Her thoughts spiraled, spinning around in endless circles, but eventually, the day's exhaustion took over. With a final exhausted breath, she sank into a deep, peaceful sleep.

Chapter 8

The familiar buzz of her phone jolted Hannah awake the next morning, breaking through the peaceful silence. Surprisingly, her nightmares or visions hadn't interrupted her sleep. For the first time in years, she had managed to fall into a tranquil, uninterrupted slumber, free from the usual unsettling dreams or visions that often haunted her. She stretched her arms above her head, letting out a long, loud yawn. Rubbing her eyes, she tried to shake off the drowsiness. But when she looked around her room, her heart skipped a beat.

Vines and flowers had erupted all over—twisting around her furniture, climbing up the walls, and even covering her drawings. The air was thick with the scent of magic, intertwining with the rich aroma of earth, while flowers bloomed in vibrant colors, unlike anything she had ever seen. Hannah blinked, struggling to believe what she was seeing. She had never seen anything like this. Her mind raced, trying to make sense of what was happening. Before she could even move, a knock echoed gently from her bedroom door.

 "Hey, sleepyhead, you're going to be late for school," Jeremy's voice called through the door.

Hannah jumped at the sound and quickly ran to the door, pressing her ear against it. "Don't worry, Dad, I'm already up," she replied.

Her heart pounded as she turned back to the vines and flowers, her pulse quickening. She reached out instinctively, trying to pull them off the walls with all her strength. But as soon as her hands touched them, more vines sprouted, winding and twisting around her fingers. A faint green glow shimmered from her skin, and panic washed over her like a tidal wave.

"Are you okay in there?" Jeremy called again, his voice ringing with concern. His words made Hannah jump, the distress of her secret pressing down on her, making it harder to breathe.

Hannah immediately stopped pulling the vines. Her many attempts to stop them from growing failed. She rushed to the door, cracked it open, and peeked out. "Hey, Dad, what's up?" she asked, trying to sound nonchalant, though her voice trembled slightly.

Jeremy stepped back when he noticed the strange green glow filling her room. His eyebrows furrowed in confusion as he tried to make sense of it. "You sure everything's okay in here?" he asked.

Hannah's mind raced again, scrambling for a quick excuse. "Yeah, I'm fine," she said, forcing a smile. "It's just my science homework giving me trouble again."

Jeremy's eyes kept darting toward Hannah's room, his gaze narrowing with suspicion, but he shrugged it off. "Okay … well, I'll be downstairs if you need anything," he said. "Your mom and Sadie just left, so I'm dropping you off at school."

As soon as her dad was out of sight, Hannah closed the door behind her, exhaling with relief. She looked back, half expecting to see the flowers and vines sprawled across the room. But, to her surprise, they weren't—not a single vine or flower in sight. Everything looked the same: her furniture was in place, the walls empty, and her drawings untouched.

Bewildered, Hannah stood there a while, trying to wrap her mind around what had just happened. However, the strange event seemed impossible, as if it never really occurred. She pushed it aside with a shake of her head and threw herself into her morning routine, hoping that whatever it was would be erased from her mind. A few minutes later, Hannah wandered into the kitchen, trying to shake off the feeling from earlier.

A few minutes later, Hannah wandered into the kitchen, still trying to shake the strange feeling from earlier. She wore her long-sleeved, round-neck tee. The shirt was black at the top, mint green in the middle, and gray at the bottom. She paired it with black leggings and black-and-white high-top sneakers, which made light taps every time she walked across the kitchen floor. Grabbing a Pop-Tart from the counter, she headed out the door and climbed into her dad's car.

The day itself felt strangely normal, like nothing had happened. The drive to school was quiet and uneventful. There were no signs of the magical vines or flowers—nothing to remind her of the weirdness of her room.

Yet, as Ms. Reza lectured about the nonfiction themes, Hannah's thoughts kept slipping away. The rhythm of her pencil tapping on her notebook matched the pounding of her heart. Her eyes drifted from the smart board to her phone, unable to stay focused. The image of the vines and flowers kept flashing in her mind, almost like they were still there, waiting to burst again. She couldn't shake the feeling that her friends wouldn't believe her if she told them. She felt she was losing her sense of reality the more she considered it. Her thoughts spiraled, her mind running around in circles. Desperate for a distraction, she took out her phone, slid it under her desk, and quickly typed a message in the group chat, hoping it would help her forget the confusion inside her.

"Can we meet after seventh period?" she typed, hoping they would sense the urgency in her message before pressing *send*.

The rest of the day dragged on in a blur. No matter how hard she tried, Hannah couldn't focus on anything but the strange things she had witnessed in her room. Finally, when the last bell rang, signaling the end of seventh period, she rushed to the courtyard, where Sydney, Zoey, Dominique, and Amber were already waiting.

"What is so important that you wanted us to meet here?" Dominique asked, her voice sharp and impatient as she crossed her arms.

Hannah scanned the courtyard, making sure no one was listening, then lowered her voice to a whisper. "Have any of you noticed anything … strange happening recently?" she asked.

The girls exchanged curious glances at Hannah, and Amber raised an eyebrow. "What do you mean?" she asked, subtly tilting her head.

Hannah hesitated for a moment before leaning in closer. "This morning, I woke up to vines and flowers growing all over my bedroom," she whispered, her voice noticeably shaking with uncertainty. "I know it sounds crazy, but I swear it's real."

The girls stared at her, confusion written across their faces. Zoey was the first to speak. "How come you're the only one who can see them?" she asked.

Hannah shook her head, feeling just as lost as the others. "I don't know … but it's like something out of a fiction novel," she explained, her mind racing.

"Wait, you're saying that this actually happened?" Sydney asked.
Hannah nodded, feeling a little bit of relief that her friends were finally starting to believe her. "The strangest part was that, after my dad knocked on my door and then left, they were completely gone," she added, her voice dropping as she thought back to the strange moment.

"Gone? Like, vanished into thin air?" Dominique asked, her eyes gleaming with surprise.

"Yeah, and the weirdest thing is … my dad didn't even see them," Hannah added.

The girls were still processing what she had said when someone interrupted them. "I thought I was the only one having this déjà vu," Nia said, walking toward them with her messy, curly hair pulled back in a high ponytail.

The girls turned to face her, surprised. "What did I miss?" Nia asked. Hannah quickly explained everything, and Nia's eyes opened wide, almost too stunned to blink. "That's crazy!" she exclaimed. "Wait … something weird happened to me this morning, too."

"What happened?" Dominique asked, her brow raised with concern. Nia paused, gathering her thoughts as she tried to find the right words. "I was blow-drying my hair when, out of nowhere, a huge gust of wind blew through my bathroom," she said, her voice wavered tentatively. "It shorted out my blow dryer. It was so weird. It was like … the wind was inside my house."

Sydney stared, her eyes clouded with perplexity. "How is that even possible? How could wind get inside your house?" she asked.

Nia shrugged as if she didn't have the answers before speaking. "I don't know," she said, her voice slightly trailing off. "It's like everything is … changing."

Amber spoke up, her voice filled with worry. "Do you think this has something to do with the magic circle in the caverns from yesterday?" she said. "I mean … I still don't understand why my necklace is connected to it."

The girls stared at Amber, unsure what to make of her statement but too distracted to dwell on it. Zoey turned away from the conversation, her body stiffening. She froze as the soft fabric of her mauve, gray, and white hoodie brushed against her hand. Her eyes rounded in panic. Her heart pounded in her chest as she quickly checked around her neck—her necklace was gone.

Without saying a word, Zoey turned and sprinted toward the forest. The others called after her, but she didn't stop. She ignored their voices, already too far ahead, cutting across a shortcut toward the trees. The girls exchanged confused glances and hurried to catch up, constantly calling out her name again. Again, Zoey didn't respond. Finally, they caught up to her. She was sitting on a big gray rock, staring off into the distance, completely lost in thought.

Dominique crossed her arms, her lips pressed tight in a frown. The sleeves of her olive-green cardigan, with its pockets, shifted as she pulled her arms closer to her chest, the velvety fabric brushing against her simple, coffee-brown, long-sleeved shirt.

"Hey, Zoey," she said, her voice firm and insistent. "If you're gonna take off like that, just remember we're not supposed to go back to the forest."

Zoey didn't respond, her view locked on the forest ahead, still distant and silent.

"Hey! I'm talking to you!" Dominique yelled.
Zoey didn't flinch or say a word. She merely stood up and walked further into the woods, her movements quick and deliberate. The girls hesitated, watching her, unsure of what she was doing, until Zoey stepped through what looked like the same invisible wall from the restricted area of the forest. Their hearts skipped a beat, and their expressions intensified in disbelief.

"Isn't that …?" Amber whimpered, her voice barely audible.
"The invisible wall from yesterday?" asked Sydney.
"I think so," Nia murmured, her eyes flying open with shock.
Before anyone could stop Zoey, Hannah stepped forward. She drew in a deep breath, her hand reaching out. Her fingers brushed the shimmering, smooth surface of the invisible wall. It felt almost like glass to the touch. With her heart racing, she followed Zoey through the barrier.

"Hannah, no!" the other girls shouted, but it was too late. Hannah blinked, curiosity flooding her mind. When her eyes opened again, she surprisingly stood in the same magical forest from yesterday. Up ahead,

Zoey was already walking back, going around in a circle, and a frustrated sigh escaped her lips.

Sydney, Dominique, Amber, and Nia quickly appeared behind them. They had all passed through the invisible wall, too.

Sydney's eyes swept over the forest's familiar surroundings. "Are we back in the same forest from yesterday?" she asked, her voice laced with hesitation.

"Looks like it," Dominique replied, scanning the area with uncertainty. Zoey groaned loudly, throwing her arms down as she marched back to the others. "I can't find my necklace," she said, her voice tainted with frustration. "It's very special to me."

The other girls caught up, their faces written with concern. Hannah gently placed a hand on her shoulder. "At least let us help you," she said.

Nia let out a loud, dramatic scoff, rolling her eyes. "*Us? In this forest?*" she said, her voice dripping with sarcasm. "Girl, in case you've forgotten, none of us have been this deep in the forest, and there's some weird invisible wall around here that pulls us into … I don't know, some kind of magical dimension or whatever."

Amber bit her lip, shifting nervously from side to side. "What if we get lost again like yesterday?" she whimpered. "What if we can't find our way back to the school?"

Dominique nodded, clearly agreeing. "I'm with them," she said, her tone firm. "This is not the time to be worrying about some necklace. We need to focus on getting out of here."

Zoey's face hardened, her eyes burning with fury as her hands clenched. "Well, finding my necklace *is* important!" she snapped. "And I'm going to find it whether you like it or not." Without waiting for a response, she stormed off, her loud footsteps echoing in the forest, shattering the peaceful tranquility around them.

Zoey stomped farther into the woods, but just as she was about to disappear between the trees, Sydney called after her, her voice loud enough for her to hear.

"Good luck getting back before dark!" she said, her tone not harsh but resolute.

Zoey stopped in her tracks, her shoulders tensing. Slowly, she turned around, her eyes darting between the others. Hannah stepped forward, her expression easing. "Zoey, we wanna help you," she said gingerly. "Please, give us a chance."

Zoey hesitated, her eyes drifting to the forest floor. She let out a hushed sigh, expressing a sense of resignation rather than frustration. Finally, she looked up at Hannah's gaze and reluctantly nodded.

"Okay," she said.
Sydney, Dominique, Nia, and Amber nodded silently, though none of them were keen to do it. Without saying much, they turned and walked off in separate directions, each starting their search for Zoey's necklace.

Hannah and Sydney ended up on the far side of the forest, where they stumbled upon the same village from yesterday. However, today, it was different. It felt deserted, silent, with no sign of life—only the loud sound of shutters slamming shut and the doors bolting quickly. It was like the whole village was trying to hide in a sudden panic, keeping something— or someone—out.

"This is giving me the creeps," Sydney muttered, her eyes scanning around with confusion. She crossed her arms. The long sleeves of her beige ribbed tunic with a crew neck and half-button front brushed against each other as she pulled herself into a hug.

Hannah couldn't help but agree with Sydney, though a heavy pit settled in her stomach as her eyes darted nervously from house to house. "We should split up here," she suggested. "We'll cover more ground and find it faster."

Sydney nodded, and the two girls went their separate ways. As Hannah wandered through the quiet village, her phone buzzed in her pocket. She pulled it out and saw a text message from her dad.

"I'm gonna be late picking you up," the text read.
Hannah typed back quickly, *"That's okay. Sydney can take me home,"* the message read. She pressed send and slipped her phone back into her pocket, her eyes drifting over the quiet line of rose granite pavement.

As she turned a corner, Hannah bumped into someone. She gasped as she stepped back, only to find herself face-to-face with a male fairy. He was thin, with pale skin and messy light brown hair. His striking blue eyes darted nervously, his breathing growing more uneven and shallow. His faded pair of brown and dark yellow wings fluttered anxiously from side to side. The moment his gaze locked on Hannah's, his eyes widened in fear.

"They're coming," he warned, his voice low yet trembling.
Hannah's eyes snapped open in confusion. "What?" she whispered, struggling to make sense of his words.

"You need to leave. Now!" the male fairy said, becoming more urgent. Before Hannah could ask who he meant, the fairy flew away in a frantic flutter, leaving her stunned and a little shaken. A strange feeling lingered in her mind—the fairy seemed strangely familiar, almost like one of her drawings. The thought sent a shiver down her spine, but she quickly brushed it off, trying to ignore the fairy's warning. Shaking her head, she pressed on through the village, her footsteps echoing in the hollowness.

As Hannah wandered deeper into the village, her heart suddenly stopped. A Korean fairy queen emerged, gracefully gliding down from the sky. Her regency purple cloak rippled in the breeze, and when she pulled back her hood, her burgundy hair caught the gentle light. Her piercing green eyes seemed to beam the entire sky itself. The queen's fair skin radiated in the sunset, bathing the village with a warm, ethereal glow.

Her gown shimmered like the night sky—rich, grape-purple chiffon with puffed sleeves that swirled as she moved. With every unearthly step, the deep V-neck caught the light, the fabric flowing down to the ground like it was alive. Her white-heeled sandals gleamed like jewels. Her tinted wings—a mesmerizing imperial purple and indigo blend—fluttered gently behind her. A sparkling amethyst circlet rested on her head, enhancing her regal presence.

Hannah stood frozen, completely mesmerized by the queen's presence. A sudden, undeniable urge to follow her gripped her. Quietly, she trailed after the fairy queen, moving carefully into another village, where fairies of all kinds were gathered in small groups, chatting and laughing. The wings of men, women, and children glowed in a spectrum of colors—muted shades of purple, pink, blue, green, red, yellow, white, and even gold and silver. Each set of wings was a stunning blend, as unique as the fairy wearing them. Hannah could not look away, wholly captivated as the village seemed to pulse with magic.

As the queen passed through, the fairies stopped what they were doing, bowing their heads in respect, one by one. In the center of the village, the queen met with two other fairy queens, who waited. Hannah's eyes broadened as she gasped in surprise. Without a second thought, she ducked behind a nearby tree, crouching down, trying to stay out of sight. She strained to hear every word of their conversation as she peered around the trunk.

The first fairy queen was African American. Her dark brown hair was pulled back into a messy bun, wispy curls framing her face. Her rich brown eyes shone like sun rays. She wore a mauve chiffon dress, its long, flowing sleeves moving like silk. The velvety fabric complemented her brown skin, radiating quiet elegance. Gold sandals adorned her feet, simple yet regal. Her wings, a beautiful ombre of white and cinnamon rose, fluttered gently in the evening air. A baroque crown sat atop her head, its dark pink tourmaline at the center, adding a royal touch.

Beside her stood the second fairy queen of Hispanic descent. Her light brown hair tumbled down her back in gentle curls, and her olive skin glistened in the sunset. Her hazel eyes were entrancing, shrouded in mystery. She wore an ocean-blue dress, its layers flowing around her feet like the waves of the sea, with lace trimming on the sleeves and hem. Royal blue ankle-strap sandals adorned her feet, adding color to her outfit. Her painted wings, a blend of Persian and azure blue, glimmered like the ocean. A sapphire crystal tiara, shaped like delicate leaves, rested atop her head, completing her captivating appearance.

"Sonia, what's the matter?" asked the first fairy queen.
The Korean fairy queen named *Sonia* let out a heavy sigh, her eyes vaguely drifting away. "Vivia captured Jacob," she said, her voice tinted with sadness. "I am afraid she will come after my son, so I sent him to my mother's."

 The second fairy queen's face tightened, her frustration building up. She threw her hands up, letting out an exasperated scoff. "Great, so now she's going to come after us next!" she exclaimed.

The first fairy queen stepped forward, her calm voice breaking through the tension. "Valentina, let us not jump to conclusions," she interjected, attempting to soothe her.

However, Valentina shook her head, worry and fear clouding her thoughts. "Onira, our world is in danger!" she yelled, her voice breaking with raw emotion. "We banished that witch for practicing dark magic, and now she's coming after us. She had the nerve to invade our kingdom and capture Javier. I had to send Gabriella to my sister's for safety. Now, I am worried sick because we have abandoned our baby girl, Alora, and we have no idea where she could be."

Valentina's fists clenched, her voice trembling with fury as she locked eyes with Onira. "May I remind you that she invaded your kingdom, too? You and Anton had to send your children away to protect them from her. You even abandoned your twin babies before she could reach them."

She turned toward Sonia, her frustration still boiling over. "And you and Jacob had to send Noelia away, too!" she shouted.

Onira stood composed and calm, her face controlled yet determined. She didn't flinch or say a word in response to Valentina's outburst. She stayed motionless, her eyes fixed on Valentina as she paced, her agitation growing with each step.

"I can't wait anymore. I need to find Alora now!" Valentina's voice cracked, tears threatening to fall from her eyes. With a firm but gentle grip, Onira grabbed her wrist, stopping her in her tracks.

"Valentina, I understand," she said. "I want to find Cecily and Astral just as much as you want to find Alora. However, we must wait until it's safe. We cannot risk everything now—not with her, the Dark Fairy Clan, and the humans involved."

Valentina gave Onira a reluctant nod, her tensed shoulders slumping as she tried to calm herself. The names *Alora, Cecily,* and *Astral* lingered in Hannah's memory as the conversation continued, their significance becoming increasingly apparent. She kept thinking that they had something to do with what was happening.

Suddenly, a chilling scream pierced the air, grabbing everyone's attention.

The hooded figure and a swarm of dark fairies descended on the village.

Hannah's eyes flared in disbelief, her breath catching in her throat. The cloaked woman, the one from her nightmare with the same black and silver-blue wings who turned Cecilia into stone, was now standing before them in reality.

The woman tossed back her cloak with a swift motion, revealing her silver-blonde hair that glowed faintly in the sunset. An unsettling coldness masked her piercing, light blue eyes, and her pale skin seemed almost angelic. Her presence was as chilling as commanding, amplified by how she wore her black trumpet V-neck dress with bell sleeves that arched around her, completing her eerie yet striking appearance.

"I am Queen Vivia, ruler of the Dark Kingdom," she proclaimed, her voice commanding yet imposing, carrying an undeniable weight of authority. "I have detained the kings and queens of each kingdom, and now I demand that you surrender *all* of your magic to me and allow me to take control of the forest. If you comply, I will spare your lives and let you serve under my dominion."

Valentina, her eyes burning with fury, stepped forward. "You dare kidnap my husband and threaten our world?!" she shouted. "You may have seized control of the other kingdoms, including mine, but you will *NEVER* take control of this forest!"

Vivia's lips curled into a chilly, mocking smile. "Your emotions mean nothing to me," she sneered dismissively. "I'm afraid you leave me no choice." She leaned in closer to one of her henchmen, her eyes glinting with dark amusement as her final words hung in the air, cold and deliberate. "Do it."

The henchman nodded and lifted his hand, signaling the dark fairies to attack. Panic and chaos spread through the village as fairies screamed and scattered, rushing to find shelter in their homes. Queen Vivia's eyes narrowed as she spotted a mother fairy and her daughter trying to escape. Fueled by her dark magic, she aimed and threw a dark orb of energy toward them.

Without thinking, Valetina's instincts took over. She rushed forward, mustering up all her magical strength to summon a celestial blue force field. The shield materialized in time, blocking the dark orb and protecting them from harm. However, Queen Vivia's magic was too powerful. The shield nearly broke as the dark energy slammed against it. Even though Valentina's arms were shaking from the pressure, she looked fiercely at the mother fairy and the daughter.

"Go, go with your mother!" Valentina cried.
The daughter hesitated, attempting to step forward, but the mother fairy pulled her back, holding her tightly.

"Your Highness—" the daughter began when Valentina interrupted her words, her voice sharp with urgency.

"Just go!" Valentina shouted.
The mother fairy quickly grabbed her daughter's hand and pulled her away. "Hurry, Janessa!" she shouted, their figures disappearing into the chaos.

There was no time for relief. As they dashed through the pavement, the dark energy pressed harder against her shield, the air crackling with power. Suddenly and unexpectedly, the force field shattered under the relentless attack. The spell struck Valentina directly, and she groaned in pain, stumbling back. Her body jerked violently before she collapsed to her knees. In an instant, she felt the coldness creeping into her skin. It hardened, turning cold and stiff as stone.

Hannah stood helplessly in horror, unable to look away. She watched Valentina's eyes dull, turning into lifeless marble while her entire body gradually became solid stone. Onira and Sonia gasped in shock. Their eyes broadened with disbelief. Before she could fully succumb to the spell, Valentina let out a last, desperate cry, but her voice was quickly silenced as her form solidified completely. The two fairy queens swiftly ducked behind a small building, hiding in the shadows, trying to avoid being seen.

Onira's gaze briefly met Queen Vivia before darting to Sonia, her face etched with urgency. "Sonia, quickly. We don't have much time," she commanded. "Go north and fly across the human world."

Sonia opened her mouth to speak, but Onira interrupted her, her eyes pleading. "Find Sylvia and Kear at the Cornerstone Church. Tell them—" she started, but she didn't finish.

Before she could finish her words, Onira was struck by a flash of dark magic as the air around her began to shimmer. She screamed in pain as her body stiffened, turning into stone, just like Valentina. Panic surged through Sonia as she let out a horrified gasp. She lifted her skirt with quick reflexes, her wings flapping frantically, trying to escape the chaos. However, two dark fairies lunged at her abruptly before she could take flight. She fought against them, but their grips were like iron around her arms.

"Your mistress! I've got her!" one of them yelled, his voice full of satisfaction.

Hannah's breathing became shallow as her eyes locked on Queen Vivia, who was now focusing her sadistic glare on Sonia. Sonia struggled relentlessly against the dark fairies, her wings flapping wildly as she grunted in effort. She met Queen Vivia's gaze, and the malicious smile on Vivia's face made Hannah's blood run cold.

With sickening happiness, Queen Vivia watched as Sonia withered in agony. Sonia let out painful screams, but they were quickly swallowed as the dark magic turned her into a lifeless statue. Hannah's hands flew to her mouth, her breath catching in her throat. She realized with horror that Cecilia had likely suffered the same fate as Sonia, Onira, and Valentina. It was like she was in danger of being crushed by the weight of it all. Just then, her attention shifted to the mother fairy and her daughter, who were still trying to escape. Janessa tripped, falling to the ground and scraping her knee.

"Janessa!" the mother fairy screamed in desperation.
A surge of determination rushed through Hannah, pressuring her to act. She emerged from her hiding place, grabbing Janessa as the dark fairy reached for her. The mother fairy swooped down in front of Hannah, despite her fear, knowing she was human. In an instant, Janessa was safe in her mother's arms.

"Run! Find somewhere safe!" Hannah said, her voice urgent.
Queen Vivia's icy sneer turned toward Hannah, a malicious smile forming at the corners of her mouth. Realizing that she was in danger made Hannah's heart skip a beat. Queen Vivia's eyes lit up with a dark flash of recognition, expanding for a second. Then, with a cold, callous smile, she raised her hand, ready to strike.

Just as she began to cast the spell, a scream suddenly pierced the air, calling her name. Sydney swooped down like lightning, throwing herself between Hannah and the oncoming dark magic. Instead, Queen Vivia's conjured orb struck the tree, splintering the wood and reverberating through the atmosphere.

"Come on!" Hannah shouted, grabbing Sydney's hand as they fled from the scene.

 Queen Vivia's eyes flashed as she whirled around in rage. She glared at one of her henchmen—an extremely pale fairy with long blond hair pulled back into a ponytail. His clear blue eyes met hers, and his wings—shaded in dark red and black—seemed to shimmer. The elaborate design of his armor, which covered him from head to toe, nearly resembled a crown.

"Lucan, find them … NOW!" she demanded.
Lucan nodded sharply, his tense face tight with determination. Without a word, he took off, the other dark fairies following close behind as they chased after Hannah and Sydney. The two girls raced through the dense forest, darting past tall trees and pushing through thick bushes, their hearts pounding as they desperately tried to outrun their pursuers.

"What *ARE* those things?!" Sydney gasped, almost running out of breath as she looked over her shoulder.

"I don't know!" Hannah yelled. "Just keep running."
Their legs burned, but they didn't stop. Fear pushed them forward, refusing to look back. They eventually slowed, tiredness heaving in their chests. It took a moment for them to notice the silence. The dense, empty forest entirely encircled them, nothing but trees and shadows endlessly in every direction.

"I think we're lost," Hannah said, catching her breath as she glanced around.

Sydney's eyes widened in fear. "I'm calling the others," she said, reaching for her phone. Her fingers were shaking as she tried to dial, but before she could press call, a cold voice suddenly stopped her. Her phone slipped from her hands, landing between her beige lace-up ankle boots with a soft thud.

"Don't *EVEN* think about running," the voice hissed.
The girls froze, fear coursing through them as they slowly turned. Lucan was standing right behind them, his eyes glowing with menace. The dark fairies circled him, surrounding them in every direction. Their hearts pounded in their chests. Sydney discreetly slipped her phone behind her, typing a hurried message with quick hands. Lucan marched forward, his dark eyes still fixed on them with contempt.

"What brings you disgusting humans to our world?" he sneered, his voice laced with disdain.

Hannah forced herself to speak despite her voice faltering shakily. The words escaped her lips, her breath catching as the panic churned inside her. "We come in peace," she said quickly. "We're trying to find something, but we got lost. We were trying to find our way back and—"

Before Hannah could finish, Sydney's quick instincts took over. With a burst of movement, she bolted to the side, trying to make a run for it. Lucan's eyes narrowed in fury, and in an instant, he raised his hand. A wave of dark energy shot toward Sydney, striking her in the chest. She stumbled back as her legs buckled. She collapsed to the ground, dazed and unable to move before she slid against a nearby tree.

"Sydney!" Hannah screamed, her voice breaking in fear.
Lucan's icy gaze turned to her, a shiver running down her spine. His gaze was sharp, almost like his eyes held her in place. She could barely move or breathe as her frightened eyes met his. Meanwhile, back in the distance, Zoey, Dominique, Amber, and Nia searched for them. Dominique's voice echoed through the trees as she called out their names, but there was no answer. Her eyes darted around the forest with growing concern as she hesitated.

"Where *did* they go?" she asked, waving her hand and shrugging her shoulders.

Zoey rolled her eyes, her voice dripping with sarcasm. "If I knew, don't you think I'd tell you?" she asked.

Then, a loud scream echoed through the forest—it was Hannah's. Their hearts pounded in distress as they rushed toward the sound, filled with anxiety. They arrived just in time to witness Lucan push Hannah toward the edge of the cliff. Her scream faded as she disappeared from view, rocks tumbling below.

"Hannah!" Amber screamed, her voice full of panic.

"Come on!" Nia yelled, her feet stomping as she and the others raced toward the cliff.

Hannah, unbeknownst to them, hadn't fallen unconscious. She had somehow managed to gather her strength as she pulled herself up after the crash. Her body ached, but she maintained her sharp, shaky breaths to calm her racing mind. Her heart beat like a drum as she stared at the steep drop beneath her. Then, she heard Dominique's voice, clear and full of fear, calling out to her.

"Hannah!" Dominique called down. "Hold on, we're coming!"

Hannah pulled her head up, her eyes meeting Dominique's from above. The urgency in her look was unmistakable. "Dominique, get out of here … now!" she shouted, her voice strained and panicked.

Dominique's brow tensed, trying to make sense of the panic in Hannah's voice. "What? What's wrong?" she yelled.

"That guy! He's right behind you!" Hannah yelled, pointing frantically over her shoulder.

Lucan emerged from the shadows, his eyes cold and full of malice. Dominique gasped, her heart skipping a beat as she froze in shock. Without warning, Lucan lunged toward her, his hands crackling with dark energy. Yet, Dominique was faster. She jumped out of the way just in time.

Before Lucan could unleash another magic orb, Zoey's voice rang out, echoing in his ears. "Hey!" she screamed, hurling a rock that struck him in the back of the head. He groaned in pain and frustration, his attention momentarily diverted as he turned to face Zoey.

"Hey, freak, over here!" Zoey shouted. "I'm right here. Come on, dude! Come and get me!"

Snarling at her taunt, Lucan focused on Zoey, his temper flaring. As he did, Dominique and Amber quickly helped Hannah to her feet. Nia rushed to Sydney, who had just regained consciousness. But Lucan wasn't done. He raised his hand, sending another wave of dark magic toward Zoey. The blast struck Zoey with force, sending her sprawling and knocking her off balance. She cried out as her foot slipped dangerously close to the edge of the cliff.

"Zoey!" Sydney called out, grabbing Zoey's hand just in time and pulling her back from the edge before they quickly rejoined the others.

Their hearts hammered as they sprinted through the forest, branches and twigs cutting through their skin as they tried to escape Lucan and his chaotic rampage. They ignored his furious shouts, growing louder behind them. As they turned a corner, Amber's foot, snug in her chestnut brown suede mid-calf snow boots, got caught on a hidden root. With a startled yelp, she stumbled forward, crashing to the ground with a loud thud, barely keeping her pink crewneck cable-knit sweater from brushing the dirt and just in time to stop her pigtails from getting tangled in the underbrush.

As she struggled to push herself up, her eyes flew open in terror—a dark fairy appeared before them. Its black aura glowed ominously as it transformed into a massive creature that looked like a wolf, only much larger, stronger, and far more terrifying.

The others snuck into the bushes, breathing rapidly and quietly. Hannah's eyes grew big as she saw Amber scoot back in fear, her face pale and her body trembling. "Amber!" she screamed, her voice tight with fear.

Armed with a long stick she'd snatched from the ground beside her, Hannah leaped from the bushes, her eyes locked firmly on the creature. Amber froze, her breath shallow, muffled whimpers escaping from her lips as she stared into the creature's glowing, ferocious eyes. With a terrifying growl, the beast lunged toward her with tremendous speed.

"Get down," Hannah hissed. Without hesitation, Hannah swung the stick, striking the creature with precision. It collapsed, knocked out cold.

"You … saved me…" she whispered, her voice in awe as she and Hannah joined the others.

The girls didn't stop. They darted through the dense underbrush, weaving between trees and bushes. Their hearts refused to stop hammering as they tried to outrun Lucan and the dark fairies. Gripping a rock in her hand, Nia quickly turned and hurled it with all her strength at one of the dark fairies. The rock struck its target, sending the fairy crashing to the ground and knocking another one off balance. Time seemed to float as they ran, unsure whether Lucan was still in the rear or if Queen Vivia had joined the chase.

Their path abruptly stopped in the middle of what seemed to be an endless forest. The cliff face ahead was too steep and the trees too dense. Despair clenched in their chests as they realized they were trapped— nowhere to run and nowhere to hide.

 "It's a dead end," Nia said.
Zoey's voice was laced with uncertainty. "What are we gonna do?" she asked, fear creeping into her words.

Before they could respond, Lucan and the dark fairies closed in on them, their expression twisted in an apparent triumph.

"Well, well," Lucan sneered. "Looks like you have nowhere to run."
Bound and brought before Queen Vivia, the girls braced themselves for the supposed fate they feared was coming. Queen Vivia's eyes gleamed with malevolence as she surveyed her captive prisoners, a cold, callous smile curving at her lips. She turned to Lucan and the other dark fairies, a look of cruel anticipation on her face.

"Perform the incantation," she commanded, her voice dark and low.
The dark fairies gathered in a circle around the girls, opening their ancient black and red books. Lucan's smile deepened, turning more sinister.

"What incantation?!" Nia demanded.
Amber struggled against her restraints, her voice trembling with fear and fury. "You won't get away with this," she screamed.

However, the dark fairies remained motionless. Their eyes were cold and empty, showing no sign of mercy as they ignored the girls' cries. The air seemed to flutter with dark energy, and a pulse of magic fired toward them. Lucan and the dark fairies chanted in unison, their words infused with a heavy and sinister power.

Just as the incantation peaked, Zoey, fueled by a surge of sheer will, headbutted one of the dark fairies holding her captive. The fairy staggered back, their concentration broken. Seizing her chance, Zoey lunged toward Lucan, but he fired a blast of dark magic that sent her crashing to the ground. She lay there, groaning and breathless, dazed but still very much alive. Bruised, battered, and unbroken, Zoey's eyes darted toward a purple spark of light under a nearby bush. It was coming from her necklace, glowing faintly.

"My necklace!" she cried out.
Zoey grabbed the necklace without thinking and hastily fastened it around her neck. The moment she did, her necklace—forgotten during the chaos—and the other girls' necklaces began to glow brightly. An enchanting aura surrounded them, humming with magic. The incantation suddenly faltered. The dark fairies froze, their concentration once again slipping. The chant they had so confidently spoken came to a sudden halt. Their fierce expressions changed to ones of confusion, their eyes ricocheting back and forth as they tried to figure out what was happening.

Chapter 9

Lucan's brow knitted tightly, his fists clenching at his sides. His mouth fell open in disbelief as he tried to understand why the incantation hadn't worked. It felt like the magic itself had turned against him. Scorching anger surged inside him, making his breath come faster and harder. His sharp, furious eyes focused on the dark fairy holding Hannah, his fury intensifying. Her black hair and blue eyes seemed to mock him, and with a snarl, he turned toward her, glaring as his fury took over.

"Why did the incantation stop?!" he bellowed, his voice booming through the forest.

The dark fairy flinched, her voice wavering with confusion. "I-I don't know. Something went wrong," she stammered.

Above them, the full moon rose, casting an eerie glow over the scene. Its silver light glinted on the ground, causing the shadows to stretch and twist unnaturally. As the moonlight touched Hannah's necklace, it started to pulse steadily, a gentle glow flickering to life. Gradually, the light grew stronger, its glow brightening as the moon's beams danced across it. Finally, the necklace shimmered with a shining green light.

Unaware of the strange power hidden within her necklace, Lucan let out an exasperated growl. He grabbed Hannah's arm and jerked her toward the center of the circle, his grip so strong and vigorous. Dark energy crackled around his hand as he prepared himself for a second attempt to turn her into a dark fairy.

But before he could cast the spell, something unexpected happened. Hannah instinctively raised her arms in front of her. In an instant, a glistening green shield erupted around her. The shockwave from the luminous barrier knocked Lucan off his feet, his spell breaking apart and vanishing into thin air. As the incantation shattered, the dark fairies behind him were also thrown back, their faces distorted in disbelief. Lucan and the others watched helplessly, stunned by the unexpected display of power. Hannah's necklace pulsed again, and to everyone's surprise, the other girls' necklaces began to glow, too, their enchanted light joining Hannah's.

"Guys, what's happening?" Amber whimpered, her eyes expanded in bewilderment.

Looking at her hand, Hannah felt a rush of power through her. A vibrant green glow aura radiated from her skin, pulsing with energy. The same fiery green that had once flashed inside her now reflected in her eyes, glowing with an intensity that matched the power within her.

The once-confident dark fairies around her now quivered in fear, sensing the dangerous force she had become. Hannah's body glowed with an intense luminescence, her green aura pulsing in sync with her rapidly beating heart, humming and growing stronger with each passing moment. Hannah's arm shot up swiftly, instinctively, the silver moonlight casting a luster across her face. Vines twisted and wrapped around the dark fairies from the ground below, ensnaring them in the air and turning them into mist.

Beside Hannah, Sydney's eyes shone a bright orange, filled with fiery energy. With a swift motion, she thrust her hands forward, and flames shot out, racing toward the dark fairies and instantly reducing them to ashes. Nia's eyes flamed a blazing pink as she lifted her arms, unleashing a fierce wind. The dark fairies tumbled through the air as it roared like a storm whipping across the forest.

The battle raged on intensely, the ground trembling like an earthquake. More vines warped and twisted, sprouting from the ground and encircling Hannah's body. In a burst of energy, the vines formed into a richly colored pair of green and chartreuse wings that erupted from her back, shimmering in the moonlight.

Not far from her, a powerful vortex of wind surrounded Nia, her ponytail whipping around in the gusts. The wind tugged at her sky blue hoodie, the sleeves marked with bold blocks of gray, black, and sky blue, making the fabric ripple in the storm. Her medium blue skinny, ripped jeans and white and black low-top sneakers with white laces stayed perfectly in place, unaffected by the swirling chaos. Despite the encompassing whirlwind, her outfit remained untouched. It was almost like the cyclone couldn't touch her. Then, a gradual blend of pink and hot pink wings unfurled from her back, glowing brightly as the wind roared around her.

Engulfed in dancing flames, Sydney felt the heat rising as orange and dark orange wings extended gracefully from her back, flaring with intensity. Lucan helplessly stood frozen, his eyes wide with disbelief as he watched Hannah, Sydney, and Nia soar by. The powers lit up the night, a blend of grace and fury as they fought with a skill that, despite their inexperience, was unmatched by anything he had ever seen.

Zoey felt a strange pulse in her hand, a familiar purple glow spreading through her fingers like electricity. As more dark fairies charged toward her, she lifted her head, her eyes glowing a mesmerizing, vibrant purple. She stretched out her arm, reaching for the fairies, connecting with the earth's essence beneath her feet, pulsing with energy. Suddenly, rocks erupted from the ground, soaring toward the fairies like arrows. The debris slammed into them with a thunderous crash, shattering their bodies into nothingness and leaving only dust in the air.

Dominique extended her hand, her eyes beaming a piercing blue. Water from a nearby stream rose, bending and twisting at her command. The water surged forward in a tremendous flood, crashing into the dark fairies and dissolving them into mist.

Amber's eyes flickered with turquoise light, and her hands glistened with the same glow. With a quick flick of her wrist, a beam of turquoise energy blasted forward, freezing the remaining dark fairies in midair. They turned into sparkling ice, their forms suspended, frozen in place.

Suddenly, icy tendrils of shimmering, frosty winds swirled around Amber, lifting her off the ground. With a sudden burst of magic, a gradient merge of turquoise and cyan wings sprouted from her back, sparkling like frozen glaciers.

At the same time, water rose, swirling around Dominique, forming mystical tendrils that danced and twirled in the air. With a surge of energy through the liquid, a transitioned pair of blue and cerulean wings materialized behind her, glittering with power.

 Zoey's feet lifted off the ground as rocks and stones whirled around her. They tangled in the air, shaping into wings glowing with rich, blazing colors of purple and lilac. With their wings humming from the power of their magic, the three girls flew together. They joined the fray with newfound strength, battling fiercely alongside Hannah, Sydney, and Nia against the relentless tide of dark fairies.

The last of the remaining dark fairies charged toward Hannah, their eyes filled with ferocious fury. Without hesitation, she quickly threw her hands out, summoning more thick vines that erupted around her from the earth. Before the fairies could even scream, the twisting vines ensnared them, dissolving them into mist.

More dark fairies appeared behind her, but Amber, with a fierce sweep of her hand, sent a blast of freezing air toward them. The fairies froze mid-flight, their bodies turning into sparkling, icy statues. Hiding behind Amber, one dark fairy hurled an orb of dark energy at her. Yet before it could hit, Sydney's fiery orb collided with it, exploding in flames and reducing the fairy to ash.

Two dark fairies charged toward Sydney with powerful force but met a surge of magic from Dominique. Water shot up in a twisting wave, crashing into the fairies and pulling them into its current. It consumed them, dissolving their bodies before they could even hit the ground.

Four more dark fairies rushed forward, preparing for a counterattack, but Nia summoned a powerful gust of wind that sent them flying through the air, reducing them into vapor before they could strike. Nia quickly turned around, her eyes narrowing as she spotted another dark fairy charging at her. Before it could reach her, Zoey stomped on the forest floor. A barrage of earth shards erupted from the ground, soaring toward the dark fairy and crushing him with a thundering crack. The earth swallowed him whole, leaving no trace behind.

Sydney's eyes bulged as she stared at her beaming wings, reflecting in the moonlight. "Whoa, I have wings!" she exclaimed.

Amber turned from side to side, feeling the weight of her wings. "So do I," she whispered, her voice filled with admiration.

Hannah blinked rapidly, trying to wrap her mind around everything. The fairies she had drawn as a little girl were no longer just drawings—they were real, standing before her eyes. The strange nightmares and visions from her childhood were undeniable, too. "I can't believe this is real," she murmured.

Nia rolled her eyes, breaking the moment. "Uh, hate to interrupt," she said, her tone sharp. "But we *really* need to get out of here."

"She's right," Dominique concurred. "We can't stay here."
Sydney looked around, confusion written across her face. "How? There's no way out of here," she said, her voice wavering with doubt.

Zoey scanned the area, her eyes catching something glistening in the distance. "Guys, look!" she yelled.

The girls turned to see it, too—the same shimmering, invisible wall blocking their path to safety.

Amber bit her lip as her eyes fluttered with doubt. "Can we make it?" she asked, her tone full of doubt.

"We have to try," Hannah declared boldly, her eyes burning with determination.

With unyielding resolve, they soared toward the invisible wall, their hearts pounding with anticipation and intentness. In a burst of energy, they pushed through, the air crackling around them with power. They neared the wall, but Lucan's fiery gaze locked onto Hannah. His sharp eyes burned with fury and spite as if consumed by his defeat. Before they could break through, dark tendrils shot from his outstretched hand, wrapping around Hannah with terrifying speed, like a spider's web capturing its prey. Her screams echoed through the forest, full of fear. The others screamed her name in desperation, but Lucan, unmoved by their cries, continued to hold her in his grip, his expression cold and remorseless.

"You're not going anywhere!" he hissed, his voice dripping with malice. Lucan's dark magic pressed down on Hannah, making her body feel heavy, as though the air held her in place. Her wings faltered as she gasped for oxygen, struggling against the tendrils. The harder she fought, the tighter they seemed to squeeze. Then, something fierce and untamed flowed within her. A bright green light started to glow from her hand, pulsing with energy. The growing power seemed to repel the tendrils, causing them to shrink and recoil. With a burst of strength, she pulled her arm free and thrust her hand forward. A green orb shot from her palm, striking Lucan in the chest with a blinding flash. It flung him backward, crashing to the ground, his black zircon amulet tumbling from his neck and landing with a muted thud.

Without wasting a second, the girls leaped into the air, their wings flapping wildly, propelling them upward. As Hannah's foot landed, it struck the amulet. At first, she didn't even notice, but a sharp crack echoed in the forest. A small pulse of dark energy ruptured the amulet, sending a wave of crackling magic rocketing through the atmosphere like a thunderstorm. The ground shook beneath them.

They turned to look back. Lucan was writhing on the ground, unleashing his painful screams of disbelief. His skin shriveled, his hair turned gray, and his face twisted in agony. Ignoring the chaos behind them, the girls flew higher, past the invisible wall, and out of the enchanted forest. They left Lucan behind, returning to their world, to Avalon High. As they landed in the safety of the school courtyard, their wings twinkled before fading into specks of light.

Dominique turned to the others, letting out a shaky, relieved exhale. "What … what just happened?" she asked.

"I think … I think we just saved ourselves," Hannah replied, her voice steady but exhausted, as if everything was finally starting to weigh heavily.

"Good thing we did," Nia said with a nervous chuckle. "I don't even wanna know what it's like to be a dark fairy."

Zoey, Sydney, and Amber nodded in agreement, their faces a mixture of lingering fear and relief. Even though they made it through, the burden of everything they'd just experienced still pressed down on them. The memory of the chaos they had escaped would not shake loose so easily. Suddenly, a beam of light wedged through the darkness. Then, a gruff voice cut through the silence, grabbing the girls' attention.

"Hey! What are you girls doing out here so late?" the security guard yelled, his brow drawn in a stern expression as he lowered his flashlight.

After a brief conversation, the girls grabbed their backpacks and exchanged tired but relieved glances as they walked into the parking lot.

The guard's severe tone eased as he saw how worn out they looked. "You girls drive safely, okay?" he advised, letting them off with a warning.

"Thanks," Zoey said, her voice low from exhaustion.
The security guard gave them a reassuring smile. "Take care now," he added, shaking his head as he turned away.

After the guard left, the girls stood silently together, sharing understanding glances before parting ways.

"I … guess we'll see you guys on Monday?" asked Sydney.
"Yeah," Dominique agreed, her voice still shaky. Amber and Nia nodded in agreement as they turned to walk away.

"Come on, I'll drive you guys home," Nia said, offering a ride to Dominique and Amber.

Hannah, Sydney, and Zoey watched Nia open her teal Jeep Renegade, parked beside a red Honda Civic. Amber slid into the back seat, Dominique climbed into the passenger seat, and Nia took the driver's seat. As they watched Nia drive off, Sydney turned to Hannah and Zoey.

"I can drive you guys home if you want," she offered.

"Sure," Hannah said, a small, tired smile forming.

"I'm in," Zoey said.

They climbed into Sydney's car, and the engine hummed to life as they pulled away. The streets stretched out in the quiet night, their silence giving them a chance to catch their breath after everything that had happened. None of them said a word during the entire drive, their eyes growing heavy with exhaustion.

When they finally reached Hannah's house, she unbuckled her seatbelt and turned to Sydney and Zoey. "Thanks for the ride," she said, her voice quiet yet still weary.

 "Anytime," Sydney replied.
"See ya," Zoey said, waving goodbye.
As Hannah watched Sydney's car disappear down the street, a sense of relief washed over her. But the moment she stepped inside, her mom's fury hung in the air like a thundercloud. Her heart sank. She knew she was in trouble. They walked into the living room, tension already simmering between them.

"Mom, I can explain," she ventured, her voice small and hesitant. Maggie's eyes narrowed, her tone sharp, woven with concern and frustration. "Can you?" she yelled. "Can you explain why you haven't answered any of your father's or my calls and messages? And why you came home hours past your curfew?"

 "You texted me?" Hannah asked, blinking in surprise.
She pulled out her phone, fumbling with it nervously. A stream of unread messages from her parents filled the screen. Her eyes grew immense as realization hit her. She'd been so caught up in the whole ordeal in the magic forest that she hadn't even noticed the messages. Biting her lip, she struggled to come up with the right words. Maggie's tone shifted, growing more scolding.

"Hannah Liliana Sumpter, if those girls are up to some kind of hazing, I swear I will—" she started to say, but Hannah interrupted her.

"Mom, they're not like that," she asserted, her voice getting louder. "Besides, I'm sixteen! I can go out and do whatever I want."

Before Maggie could respond, footsteps echoed down the hall, followed by the creak of a door opening. Sadie appeared at the top of the stairs, leaning over the railing. "Is Hannah in trouble?" she asked, her voice dripping with mischievous curiosity.

Hannah and Maggie responded to her simultaneously, giving Sadie a look that clearly said, "Stay out of it." Sadie just shrugged, her lips pressing together in a slight frown before returning to her room.

A moment of tense silence hung in the air between them. Maggie took an unsteady breath, her voice mellowing but still firm. "Listen, I know you're sixteen, but you are still my daughter," she advised, her eyes narrowing with seriousness. "I can't stop you from growing up too fast. If you plan to go out somewhere, *please* text me or your father. Don't let Caroline's disappearance drive you to rebel like this. Understand?"

Hannah nodded, her mind swirling with her mom's words as guilt rose in her chest. "Yeah, Mom. I understand," she said meekly, her voice barely a whisper.

Maggie stepped forward and gently kissed Hannah on her forehead, a tiny comfort provided by the warmth of her touch. Without another word, Hannah watched as her mom walked up the stairs, leaving her alone in the living room. Once the coast was clear, she settled on the couch, letting out a deep breath as she sank into the squishy cushions. Pulling out her phone, she quickly typed a message to the group chat, her mind still racing over everything that had happened.

"Meet me at my house tomorrow: 2619 Freemont St., Avalon, MO, 64159," the text read before Hannah hit send.

The next day, the girls gathered at Hannah's house, recounting last night's strange and confusing events: Lucan, the dark fairies, and Queen Vivia. Zoey's eyes scanned the living room, narrowing as she glanced around. "Is there anyone else here?" she asked, her voice low.

Looking around the room, Hannah let out a tired sigh as her shoulders slumped a little. "Nobody's here except my sister. We can go outside to the patio," she said, leading the way through the screen door and onto the patio.

Hannah, Zoey, Amber, and Nia settled into the comfy black wicker chairs, the cool rattan gently brushing against their skin before they relaxed into the softness of the cushions. The matching black table gleamed in the afternoon sunlight, its smooth surface warming up as the sun hit it, leaving Sydney and Dominique standing.

Sydney didn't hesitate to jump back into the conversation. "Okay, seriously—what *actually* happened to us? How did we *suddenly* get these powers?" she asked.

Hannah swept a strand of her hair behind her ear, her gaze distant as she recalled the events from last night. "When that guy lunged at me, it felt like something was protecting me," she explained in a subdued tone. "It was like a force field, and then I could control vines and plants around me."

Zoey's eyes were huge as she nodded. "I found myself manipulating rocks or something," she added, her voice trailing off as she struggled to understand it.

"Then, I had the power to control the wind," Nia interjected.
Dominique looked down at her hands, struggling to find the words. "I could manipulate water," she said, her voice steady but with a hint of skepticism. "Like I could make it bend and move however I wanted."

Amber moved uneasily, her eyes flickering anxiously around the group. "I … I could manipulate ice," she murmured.
Sydney hesitated for a moment, biting her lip before speaking. "And I could control fire," she admitted, her voice barely a whisper.

Amber's eyes grew round with surprise. "And I … grew wings. Did it happen to you guys, too?" she asked, her voice a mixture of astonishment and curiosity.

The girls looked at one another, nodding in agreement. Nia was the first to speak up. "Yeah, and it was like I was in charge. Like I had total control over what I was doing," she said.

Sydney's eyes grew round like saucers with sudden realization. "Yeah, it happened to me, too. It's like w-we're ... w-we're ... " she trailed off, searching for the right words.

 "We're ... fairies, right?" Zoey said, finishing the thought with a sly grin on her face.

Dominique scoffed, crossing her arms. "Oh, come on, that's ridiculous," she said, rolling her eyes. "Fairies don't exist. They're make-believe."

Zoey pressed on, her eyes expanding with excitement as she spoke. "I'm just saying. What if that tree gave us these powers?" she paused, a new thought flashing in her mind. "What if we're the chosen ones?"

Dominique's arms tightened across her chest. "First off, like I said, fairies *do not* exist. Second, why would they live in this part of the forest? And third, what makes you think we're the chosen ones?" she demanded.

Undaunted by Dominique's cynicism, Zoey shrugged and flashed her grin again. "Maybe because of our necklaces?" she suggested.

Dominique scoffed again, shaking her head. "Oh, please, who's going to believe this kind of stuff?" she questioned again, her voice rising with disbelief.

A strange pull nudged Hannah to speak up, breaking the silence. "I would," she said quietly.

The girls turned to her, surprise and concern written all over their faces. Hannah paused, her gaze distant as she took a deep breath. Slowly, she continued, her voice barely above a whisper. "I think ... I think I've dreamed of this place before," she explained, her words lingering in the air.

"What do you mean?" Nia asked, her curiosity piquing in her eyes. Hannah took another slow breath, gathering her thoughts before speaking again. "Ever since Caroline disappeared, I've been having nightmares about her," she said. "But it's not just that … I keep having these weird visions about her and … other things."

"What other things?" Amber asked, her gaze expressing concern. Hannah hesitated for a moment, swallowing hard as she continued. "This place, the forest … It's full of trees and bushes," she paused. "There are villages and a lot of water. When we passed through that invisible wall, it felt like … like … I'd been there before. I can't get that image out of my head."

Her eyes turned into saucers as if the realization had just dawned on her. Slowly, she turned to face the others, her face almost pale. "That forest … That forest was in my nightmares," she said, her voice trembling under the significance of her words.

Sydney's brow drew together as she tilted her head. "How is that even possible?" she asked.

Hannah shook her head and bit her lower lip, her eyes briefly sullen. "I don't know. That's what I'm trying to figure out," she said, her voice composed, though a trace of doubt lingered in her eyes.

The girls exchanged glances, and a heavy silence fell over them as they all processed what Hannah had said.

"There's something else," Hannah added quietly. "I had a vision of this woman. She looked like a fairy queen, with a crown and a green dress. Then, I had a nightmare about another fairy queen. She lost a battle to someone wearing a black cloak, and the cloaked woman turned her into stone. Her name … I think it was Celia or Cecilia. Whenever I have a vision or a nightmare, I sketch what I see."

Zoey's face lightened, and she extended her hand, her voice brimming with sympathy. "Geez, I'm so sorry," she murmured, her eyes filled with understanding.

Hannah smiled subtly, feeling the warmth gradually spread through her chest. As the girls closed around her, their shoulders brushed, and their soft breaths created a quiet sense of comfort. She could feel their silent support of solidarity wrapped around her like a heated cloak, relieving the anxiety in her chest.

Nia shifted, her expression turning serious as her eyes bounced around. "So what do we do now?" she asked.

The girls exchanged glances, their eyes blinking from one to another, uncertainty filling the silence. Finally, Hannah spoke up, her voice full of quiet determination. "I wanna learn more about this forest," she said.

Dominique raised an eyebrow, disbelief flickering across her face. "Are you serious?" she asked, her skepticism resurfacing.

Hannah nodded, her expression unwavering. "If that part of that forest is somehow connected to my dreams, then I wanna know how … and why," she said, her voice growing stronger with conviction.

"I hate to say this, but Hannah's right," Sydney agreed. "I want to know, too. I also wanna figure out what that magic circle really means and how it's connected to our necklaces."

The other girls hesitated, uncertainty still lingering in the air. Zoey broke the silence first, her eyes flashing with a quiet resolve as she straightened her back and stood tall. "If you guys are serious about this, I'm in," she said, her voice steady and sure.

Nia looked between them, her face torn but resolute. "Count me in, too," she said.

"Ditto," Amber declared, her voice once hesitant but becoming mightier as her eyes lit up with curiosity.

The girls nodded in unison, their gazes locked for a moment before turning to Dominique, their silent plea clear. Indecision crossed Dominique's face as her shoulders stiffened and her eyes flitted between them. She didn't want to get involved, but their hopeful looks made her hesitate. Her mind urged her to walk away, but a tiny spark of curiosity pushed her forward, the need for answers growing stronger with each passing minute.

"Okay, I'll do it," she sighed, resigned.
As Dominique's words left her mouth, a silent sense of unity washed over the group. It was like the weight of their newfound knowledge had bound them together, making everything feel more real, more genuine. Hannah's lips transformed into a grateful smile, her heart swelling with appreciation for the support of her friends, even despite Dominique's reluctance.

"Thanks, guys," she said.
"So, what now?" asked Sydney, leaning forward, her eyes scanning the group eagerly.

Hannah turned to Dominique, her expression serious. "Do you think you can find some articles? Articles, books, something about the forest, the fairies, the magic circle? Anything?" she asked.

Dominique let out another reluctant sigh, biting her lip. "I've got a violin lesson tonight … but …" she trailed off, her eyes slightly darting to the side. "I'll see what I can do."

"Okay, we'll meet tomorrow during Panther Time in the courtyard," Hannah said, holding her hand. "Like I said, we *can't tell anyone* about our powers or what happened. Understand?"

The girls nodded quietly, their hands stacked on each other in a silent but impactful promise. It wasn't just a gesture. It was something more compelling—a friendship forged in that simple touch. Above them, the sky darkened, painting gold, pink, and blue shades. The colors grew deeper and more vibrant as night extended across the horizon. The air turned cooler, and shadows grew longer, creeping slowly toward the neighborhood. One by one, the girls started to drift off in different directions, the gravity of their secret still bearing down on the simplicity. Hannah lingered by the porch light, her shoulder leaning against the doorframe. She watched as Zoey turned back, her eyes sparkling with mischief.

"Remember what I said?" she asked softly.
A sly smirk curved at Zoey's lips, and her mischievous gaze met Hannah's serious, pleading one. "Don't worry," she replied, her voice thick with sarcasm. "Don't tell anyone because no one is going to believe us. And if we do, they'll think we're outcasts or freaks."

Hannah gave Zoey a modest smile and nodded slightly. As Nia's car disappeared down the street, the rest of the group split up. Dominique and Amber climbed into Sydney's car, the engine revving to life, while Zoey hopped onto her purple skateboard and sped off, her wheels clicking against the pavement. Hannah watched them leave, her smile remaining as she closed the door.

Later that night, after slipping into her gray short-sleeved tee and mint green pajama pants, Hannah crawled into bed. The cool water soothed her dry throat as she sipped slowly from her glass cup, but her mind was far from calm. The conversation from earlier still replayed in her head. Fatigue tugged at her eyelids, urging her to sleep, but no matter how hard she tried to fight it, the nagging restlessness wouldn't let go.

Then, her eyes landed on her drawings, a strange pull urging her to get up. Slowly, she climbed out of bed, her curiosity piqued. She leaned in closer, studying the intricate details of each drawing. Then suddenly, a flash of Queen Vivia's face appeared in her mind, catching her off guard. She shook her head, pushed the image aside, and tried to focus again on the drawings in front of her.

Her gaze landed on one picture—a dark fairy queen wearing a black trumpet V-neck dress with flowing bell sleeves. Her silver-blonde hair cascaded elegantly around her pale face, and her light blue eyes seemed to pierce through the paper, as if staring directly into her soul. The dark fairy queen stood beside a majestic white-pink pegasus with wings spread wide.

Momentarily hesitating, Hannah reached out and carefully took the drawing down. She studied it closely, her heart skipping a beat as a wave of recognition washed over her like a rush of cold air. The fairy queen in the drawing resembled Queen Vivia from the magic forest.

Everything instantly clicked into place—the mysterious figure in her drawing *was* Queen Vivia. Hannah's eyes grew in size, and a chill ran down her spine as her hand traced the lines of the drawing. As her fingertips brushed the paper, its smooth texture felt almost alive, like the drawing was stirring under her touch.

The following day at Avalon High, Nia, Amber, and Zoey gathered in the courtyard, glancing around as they waited for Hannah, Sydney, and Dominique. Amber's eyes were glued to her phone as she tried to type a text message on the group chat. At the same time, her other hand pushed her dark turquoise sequin laptop backpack with a marble pattern. Nia's eyes enlarged when she saw Zoey devouring what looked like a jar of kimchi. The loud crunching made her crinkle her brow with disbelief and confusion.

"Girl, what *is* that?" she asked.

"It's kimchi," Zoey replied with a mischievous grin, pulling out a piece and letting the sauce drip down her hand. "Want a taste? Perfect for breakfast, lunch, and dinner."

"I just had a frittata," Amber muttered.
Nia waved her hand in front of her face, backing away. "I'll pass," she refused, clearly not interested. Zoey shrugged, grinning as she took another bite. "Your loss," she teased.

Just then, Hannah and Sydney arrived, and the girls greeted each other with a hint of thrill. Sydney glanced around before leaning in. "Is the coast clear?" she asked in a hushed voice.

Nia quickly scanned the area and nodded. "You're good," she whispered back.

 Sydney gave a silent nod to Hannah, signaling her to pull out the drawing, now folded and crumpled from her jean jacket pocket. Hannah carefully unfolded it and laid it flat on the table. The girls leaned in, eyes brimming with curiosity as they examined the drawing's intricate details.

Chapter 10

Zoey's finger hovered over the dark fairy queen in the drawing. She narrowed her eyes at the image, a frown pulling at her mouth. "Who's that?" she asked, her voice inquisitive.

Hannah's face lit up, her eyes dancing with recognition. "That's the woman from the other day … and from my dreams," she replied.

The others froze. Zoey, Nia, Amber, and all looked at each other with saucer-like eyes, their expressions displaying a mix of surprise and perplexity.

"What?" Nia blurted out.
"Are you sure?" Amber asked, leaning closer, her brow raised.
Hannah nodded slowly, her gaze refusing to leave the image as if she couldn't look away. "Positive," she said. "Her hair, her wings, her outfit—everything. It's her, I'm sure of it."

Zoey shuddered, her shoulders tensing. "Ugh, she looks … creepy just by looking at her," she said, her voice tight, like the image was already haunting her.

"And that's not all," Hannah continued. "I remember her name—Vivia. I also remember she was voted for banishment."

A frown tugged at the corners of Sydney's mouth as her brow gathered in thought. "But why? Why was she voted for banishment?" she asked, her voice full of curiosity.

Before anyone could respond, Dominique's loud voice cut through the air, making them all jump. "It's a good thing I've got all the answers," she said, approaching them, a stack of papers clutched tightly in her hand.

"Turns out there's more information than just about fairies and the magic circle." Dominique pulled out a printed article from Wikipedia, its edges crisp yet slightly curled from being folded. The girls leaned in closely, their eyes stretched with attentiveness.

At the top of the article, the title, *Avalon, Missouri,* was boldly printed in black letters. A small label read *Start-Class underneath,* meaning it was still a work in progress. Just below, a navigation box lined with links led to related articles, like "The Avalon Forest" and "List of Cities in Missouri." As she skipped the introduction and the table of contents, Dominique's finger skimmed down the page, landing on the history and the geography section.

"According to this," she began, her voice steady with interest, her eyes shifting from the others to the article. "Avalon was once a realm of fairies, sprites, and pegasi before it officially became a city. In the heart of the magical Avalon Forest, six kingdoms flourished, each ruled by a king and queen."

Dominique paused for a moment, her eyes still scanning the article. "Here's a list of the kingdoms," she said. "King Seth and Queen Ariah ruled the Emerald Kingdom. King Aaron and Queen Cecilia ruled the Topaz Kingdom. King Jacob and Queen Sonia ruled the Amethyst Kingdom. King Javier and Queen Valentina ruled the Sapphire Kingdom. King Reginald and Queen Stella ruled the Aqua Kingdom. And lastly, King Anton and Queen Onira ruled the Tourmal Kingdom."

She took a breath before continuing. "King Seth and Queen Ariah had two daughters, Katarina and Eliana. King Aaron and Queen Cecilia had two daughters, Tiara and Yasmeene. King Jacob and Queen Sonia had two children—a son, Daniel, and a daughter, Noelia. King Javier and Queen Valentina had two daughters, Gabriella and Alora. King Reginald and Queen Stella had a daughter named Sabina. And King Anton and Queen Onira had four children: a daughter, Idasia, a son, Brandon, and twins named Astral and Cecily."

As Dominique's words settled in, Hannah leaned in closer to the article, her eyes locked onto the pictures of the royal families. She pointed to the images of Sonia, Valentina, and Onira. "These are the women I saw the other day," she remarked quietly, her voice barely above a whisper. Then, her finger gestured toward the pictures of Ariah and Cecilia. "These were the ones that were from my dreams and visions."

Sydney's eyes expanded in intrigue as her brow scrunched. "Wait, what about the magic circle?" she asked.

Dominique continued scrolling, her finger tracing a particular paragraph before she read aloud again. "Twelve guardians of each kingdom used the magic circle, each aligned with a gem of great power: diamond, emerald, alexandrite, ruby, peridot, sapphire, tourmaline, citrine, topaz, garnet, amethyst, and aquamarine. To protect their kingdoms and the fairy realm, they used the circle to create an invisible barrier as a gateway between the human and the fairy worlds."

Everyone exchanged glances, their eyes huge with a mixture of bewilderment and intrigue.

"Okay, so what about this *Queen Vivia*?" Zoey asked, her voice unable to contain her curiosity.

"I was getting to that," Dominique replied, adopting a tone of authority as she continued reading.

Her eyes blinked over the following paragraph, her finger tapping on the page's smooth surface. "It says here that a long time ago, Vivia was once the guardian of the Emerald Kingdom. But after the birth of King Seth and Queen Ariah's second daughter, she was caught practicing dark magic," Dominique explained, her voice growing darker. "As punishment, she was voted for banishment and replaced by another guardian."

The room went silent for a moment. Dominique's eyes never left the page as she read the next line.

 "Consumed by bitterness and rage, Vivia's hatred toward fairies and humans intensified. Seeking vengeance, she led her dark fairy clan to invade the Avalon Forest."

Dominique's voice grew heavier with each word. "In the aftermath, the kings and queens from each kingdom were forced to send their children away to the human world for their safety, including their younger ones. After they were gone, Queen Vivia captured some kings and queens, drained their powers, and turned them into stone statues. She kept them as trophies, trapped forever in their stone forms."

Zoey's jaw dropped, and her eyes flared in surprise. "I'm sorry I asked," she uttered in dismay.

"Hang on, how come it mentions only twelve gems in the magic circle and not the other six kingdoms?" Nia asked.

Dominique shrugged her shoulders, skimming through the pages. "It doesn't say," she said. "Maybe the kingdoms are forgotten … or there's no info yet?"

"Or maybe they just forgot to add that part?" Amber suggested, glancing at the article.

Zoey let out a scoff, rolling her eyes. "Come on, Amber. Wikipedia is the best internet source. There's no way they'd miss something like that. I know because I use it all the time," she said.

The girls exchanged perplexed glances with puckered brows as they attempted to comprehend what Zoey had just said.

"It's true," Zoey insisted with a nod.

Hannah chimed in, her voice eager and full of determination. "True or not, I want to know more about the fairies. Not just from my dreams, but why are they living in the forest? I say we meet back at my house after class and find out more about them," she suggested.

Sydney's phone buzzed in her backpack pocket, and she quickly glanced at the screen. Her eyes landed on a text message from the soccer group chat. She mouthed, "Shoot," then turned to the others with an apologetic look. "I don't think I can make it," she said. "I have soccer practice after class, but I'll try to meet up with you guys later."

Hannah nodded in understanding. "Okay," she replied, her voice becoming calmer and reassuring. Just as Sydney turned to leave, something sparked in Hannah's head. "Wait, I have an idea!"

Hannah pulled out her phone and opened their group chat, tapping the *Info* button. She scrolled down to the *Notes* section and quickly typed out two categories: *Danger* and *To Meet*. Under *Danger*, she added her name, along with the three emojis: a green heart, a Taurus symbol, and two exclamation points. Then, under *To Meet*, she did the same—this time adding the same green heart, the Taurus symbol emoji, and a house emoji.

"I need you guys to use the emojis as a code in case someone's in danger or if you want to meet up," Hannah explained.

The other girls followed her lead, adding their names, heart colors, zodiac signs, exclamation points, and house emojis.

"So, how does it work?" Amber asked, raising her hand.
"Simple," Hannah replied. With quick fingers, she typed a message to the group chat. All around her, phones buzzed, each with a different ringtone ringing through the air. The message—a green heart, a Taurus symbol, and two exclamation points—lit up brightly on the other girls' screens.

"If anyone's in trouble, send in your signal," Hannah continued, her eyes narrowing with steely resolve.

The girls nodded, their expressions set, eyes meeting Hannah's with unspoken understanding.

"I gotta go," Sydney said, putting her phone back into her backpack. "I'll see you guys later."

As Sydney walked off, the other girls turned to Hannah.
"So … what time do you want us to meet?" Nia asked, the silence hanging in the air.

Hannah looked at the clock on her phone, then shifted her focus to the others. "Let's meet at 4:30," she said.

As the sun set, the air grew cooler, and shadows stretched across Hannah's house. The bright blue sky faded, replaced by purple, pink, and orange as the last of daylight slipped away. Hannah descended the stairs, clutching her green MacBook Pro in her hand. She made her way to the living room and settled onto the couch, the warmth of the comfy cushions welcoming her. She opened her laptop, her fingers hovering over the keys as she typed in her username and password. Just as the screen flickered to life, revealing her wallpaper, a knock echoed through the door. Hannah's breath caught in surprise as she jolted upright, her heart skipping a beat.

She quickly crossed the room to answer it. Zoey, Dominique, Amber, and Nia stepped inside, and she led them toward the living room.

"I found out more about the six kingdoms," Dominique exclaimed. "Each kingdom's magic connects to its element, and the gemstones are the key."

Hannah leaned forward, her brow furrowed in concentration. "Okay, and what about our powers?" she pressed, her voice sharp with curiosity.

"Same thing," Dominique confirmed, pointing to the article. "The

Emerald Kingdom is nature, the Topaz Kingdom is fire, the Amethyst Kingdom is earth, the Sapphire Kingdom is water, the Aqua Kingdom is ice, and the Tourmal Kingdom is air."

The girls gathered around, leaning in closer, their gazes glued on the vibrant images of each kingdom and its corresponding gemstone.

"And that's not all," Dominique continued. "The emerald stands for royalty and patience, the topaz for truth and honesty, the amethyst for humility and sincerity, the sapphire for loyalty and virtue, the aquamarine for resilience and bravery, and the tourmaline for creativity and wisdom."

"What does this have to do with fairies in the forest?" Nia asked, her voice tainted with anxious curiosity.

Dominique pulled out the same Wikipedia article from earlier, flipping through the pages as her expression grew serious. "The fairies are real," she explained. "But they stay hidden because of the dark fairies."

Hannah's mind drifted as she tuned out the conversation, her eyes growing bigger as the fairy's warning flashed before her. Then, a sudden realization dawned on her. "That's what he was trying to warn me about," she murmured.

The others glanced at each other, their eyebrows raising in unison. Amber blinked a few times, her eyes expansive. "What?" she blurted out, her voice thick with confusion.

Hannah took a deep breath, her eyes locking with the others, the fairy's warning still heavy in her chest. "After Sydney and I split up, I turned a corner and—" she paused, unsure how to explain. "I … ran into a fairy, and the way he looked at me, it was like he was scared of something … or someone."

Dominique raised an eyebrow, her voice filled with disbelief. "A fairy?"

she asked.

Hannah nodded slowly. "Yeah, and … he was … trying to warn me about something," she explained, her voice barely above a whisper.

"What? What did he say?" Nia demanded impatiently.
Hannah's voice trembled as she recalled the ominous words. "He said, *'They're coming. You need to leave. Now!'*" she said, her gaze intense with unease.

A chill rippled through the group—the depth of Hannah's words hung in the air. Zoey's eyes bulged with astonishment, her mouth slightly open in shock. "Is he talking about the dark fairy clan?" she gasped.

Dominique shook her head, her eyes moving back to the article. "It's not just the dark fairy clan," she explained, her voice barely trembling. "Another reason the fairies stay hidden is because of Queen Vivia … and the dangers of the human world."

The girls exchanged stunned looks, their faces pale as they processed the frightful revelation. Confusion and disbelief flashed in their expressions as they struggled to understand what they heard.

Meanwhile, at Avalon High, Sydney raced across the soccer field, her orange and gray cleats pounding against the turf as she skillfully maneuvered through her teammates. The sharp thwack of the ball kicked by each player echoed around her, their movements blending into the fast-paced rhythm. She dodged past a defender wearing an orange scrimmage vest, her green T-shirt clinging to her as she shifted directions. With a swift kick, she sent the ball soaring toward the goal. To her relief, her powers didn't interfere at all during practice, sending a rush of calm over her.

The coach's whistle blew, the sharp, high-pitched sound cutting through the air. "Everybody in!" she called, her loud voice echoing across the field. In a flash, the girls were huddled around her, their cleats scuffing the turf.

"Great work, everyone!" the coach cheered. "Keep that energy up when we go against South Central. Remember, teamwork makes the dream work. If one of us fails, we all fail."

With hands stacked on each other, the coach stepped forward, her baby blue eyes scanning each player. "WHO ARE WE?!" she shouted, her voice booming across the field.

"PANTHERS!" the girls responded in unison.
"I SAID, WHO ARE WE?!" the coach repeated, her voice growing louder now, her eyes blazing with energy.

"PANTHERS!" the girls cried.
"I CAN'T HEAR YOU!" the coach bellowed, unleashing a powerful wave of energy from the top of her lungs.
"PANTHERS!!" the girls screamed, their battle cry echoing through the air, bursting with energy.

"All right, see you next week! Great job, ladies," the coach said before dismissing them and turning to Sydney. "Especially you, Sydney!"

As the girls made their way to the locker room, they showered Sydney with praise, their voices resonating. "Good job, Syd!" and "See you next week, Sydney," they called out with broad smiles.

When Sydney reached her locker, she pulled off her cleats and slipped on her comfy white slingback sports sandals. Minutes ticked by, and soon, Sydney found herself alone in the locker room. She pulled on her royal purple hoodie with the panther's logo—the same one she'd lent to Hannah after Heather and her friends had deliberately crashed into her from behind, spilling her milkshake all over her shirt and jean jacket. After removing her black ponytail holder, Sydney's hair fell loose around her shoulders, delicately contouring her face.

Sydney navigated through the narrow, winding hallways of the locker room, her eyes glued to her phone. Her fingers flew across the screen, rapidly typing a message in the group chat. The clatter of lockers slamming shut and distant laughter faded into the background, drowned out by the rhythm of her thumbs. Then, a loud thud broke the silence, making Sydney jump and snap out of her trance. The lights flickered and then went out completely, plunging the room into darkness. A cold shiver ran down her spine, and her heart started racing in her chest. She took a hesitant step forward, her eyes darting around, trying to make out anything in the dark.

"Hello?" she called out, her voice slightly trembling.
Footsteps reverberated from the depths of the locker room, followed by whispers—barely audible but growing louder with every passing step. Sydney's heart raced in her chest, thumping so hard it might burst. The footsteps and whispers were getting closer—too close. Then, all of a sudden, everything went quiet, and Sydney's shallow breaths slowed. As she rounded a corner, a dark, swirling ball of energy shot toward her. She barely dodged it in time, crashing to the floor with a thump.

For a moment, everything was blurry. Then, a familiar face hovered above her—Lucan. His dark eyes glowed with an ominous crimson light before fading back to blue, and a wicked smile curved on his lips.

"It is a pleasure to see you again," he taunted.
As Sydney met Lucan's gaze, a chill crawled up her spine, her breath almost caught in her throat. "W-what are you doing here?" she gasped, her voice shaking as she scrambled up. "How did you find me?"

Lucan's smirk deepened, sending an icy wave of fear through her—a feeling of helplessness and isolation. "Let's just say ..." he said, his words dripping with menace. "Queen Vivia has her ways of finding those she ...

deems deserving of her attention."

Sydney's body went cold, her knees trembling like jelly. She was trapped by herself, and the fear was closing in, making it hard to breathe.

Lucan let out a cruel laugh. "Oh, allow me to introduce myself," he said. "I am Lucan. The one who is going to lead you straight to your end."

Without thinking, Sydney pushed herself to her feet, backing away. Her eyes locked onto Lucan's hand as it scraped across the lockers with a harsh screech. The sound resonated down the hall, making her skin crawl.

"Okay, Lucan," she began, her sharp voice trembled slightly. "You don't have to do this. You can just let me go. My parents and friends are worried about me. They'll notice I haven't called."

Lucan let out another mocking laugh, his dark aura pulsing with malevolence. The surrounding air seemed to grow heavier, like something was closing in. "Do you really think I would let you escape? Especially after you escaped from me?" he sneered.

Sydney's eyes dropped to the floor, noticing the faint, luminous light of Lucan's other hand. A knot twisted in her stomach. "You're right," she whispered, swallowing hard. "We shouldn't have done that."

A surge of tenacity ignited inside her as she quickly hid her hand behind her back, though the orange glow still shone faintly. "But please, don't do this," she pleaded, her voice shuddering but firm. "Because if you do, there's no turning back."

Lucan's smirk intensified, his eyes tightening with dark intent. "I think I'll start right where my spell left off when you crashed into that tree," he snickered.

As Lucan took another step toward her, Sydney's eyes flickered, her mind racing for a way out. Sweat clung to her skin, panic rising as she struggled to think clearly. Then, her gaze darted to the right—a signal for hope. "Coach Menzer?" she shouted, resonating through the empty hallway.

Lucan's gaze followed her, and in an instant, Sydney hurled a blazing orb of energy at him. It struck him in the chest, knocking him off his feet with a bang. Adrenaline surged through her as she broke into a sprint, not looking back. Lucan's anguished screams rang through the hallway, but Sydney blocked them out, her focus solely on escaping. Her heart raced as she fumbled for her phone, fingers shaking as she typed. She sent her distress signal with one final push: an orange heart, a Sagittarius symbol, and two exclamation points. The message went through—her plea for help was out.

Back at Hannah's house, Zoey, Dominique, Amber, and Nia sat in the living room, glued to the articles on Hannah's MacBook Pro and Dominique's moonlight-blue HP laptop. They were buried in their research about Avalon and the Avalon Forest, scrolling through the pages of information. In the kitchen, Hannah poured five glasses of ice water, the liquid splashing into each one. She carefully placed the glasses onto an elegant gray marble acrylic tray, but her mind was lost in thought.

The article Dominique had shown earlier—the one about Avalon—kept replaying in her mind, especially the picture of King Seth, Queen Ariah, Princess Katarina, and Princess Eliana. But it was Princess Eliana who mostly lingered in her thoughts. The image of the baby, wrapped in an olive green blanket and gently held in a gray wicker basket, wouldn't leave her. It almost felt like the visions were coming back to her, though it seemed just a coincidence. Then, something struck her the most: the golden necklace with an emerald and a Taurus sign hanging from it. Hannah couldn't stop thinking about it. Her fingers instinctively touched her necklace, almost precisely like Eliana's.

Finally, Hannah snapped back to reality. She carefully arranged the glasses on the tray, but her gaze drifted to the wall hurriedly before returning to her necklace. Her fingers gently stroked the sleek surface of the emerald and the Taurus sign as numerous questions filled her mind. She wondered if the necklace truly belonged to Princess Eliana and if Eliana was still out there. It could be a possibility that she's alive, or she could have vanished forever. The uncertainty hung over her shoulders.

She pushed the thoughts aside and carried the tray to the living room, trying to shake off the uneasy feeling. "I thought you guys could use this," she said, handing out the drinks.

Zoey looked up, letting out a dry and weary laugh. "Finally," she responded. "My mouth was about to turn into a desert."

The girls smiled back at Hannah, their eyes sparkling with gratitude as they took their glasses, savoring the quiet moment. Zoey finished hers first, setting her glass down with a soft thump. Her fingers tapped restlessly on the edge, and she exhaled a long breath. Glancing toward the door, she stood up and threw her burgundy graphic hoodie over her head. The white rose heart and wings graphic design on the front stood out boldly against the fabric.

"Well, if you guys need me, I'll be out on the patio," she said, her voice flat, like she didn't care if anyone heard or responded.

Hannah watched Zoey head for the kitchen door and out to the patio, then turned her gaze to Dominique. "You know," she began. "I've never met someone extremely smart."

Dominique stiffened, her hand slipping away from her laptop. "Well, I wouldn't say *I'm* the smartest. Although many people seem to think so," she said hesitantly. "It's just … a lot of people misunderstand me."

"What do you mean?" Nia asked, tilting her head.
Dominique took a deep breath before speaking. "When I was little," she

explained, "I got picked on for being smarter than everyone else. They called me *Little Miss Perfect* because of my good grades, violin skills, and photographic memory."

"You have a photographic memory?" Amber giggled, her eyes exuding kindness and sincerity.

Dominique brushed a strand of hair behind her ear, her gaze dropping to the floor. "Yeah, I got it from my mom," she chuckled.

The girls giggled, and the sound helped lift some of the burden off Dominique's shoulders, easing her anxiety. Sensing her discomfort, Hannah gave her a tiny, reassuring smile and nudged her shoulder gently. "Okay," she said soothingly. "If you really think we'll misunderstand you or your intelligence, tell us what else you found in the article."

Dominique drew in a large breath, feeling a little more at ease. "Well … at the age of sixteen, a fairy princess is expected to get their wings and powers based on their virtue," she explained, her voice growing more confident.

The girls exchanged easy smiles, with Hannah's the most genuine, offering reassurance without a word. "See? We're not gonna judge or misunderstand you," she said. "We love your ideas and appreciate your smarts. Just be glad you have us."

Dominique smiled back, feeling a sense of affection and belonging within the group. Strangely enough, she didn't feel so alone anymore.

Suddenly, the kitchen door burst open, letting in a rush of cool air as Zoey rushed in, her face pale with panic. "Guys, Sydney's in trouble!" she exclaimed, her voice full of urgency.

Hannah and Nia leaped to their feet, eyes like saucers.

"What?!" Amber and Dominique shouted.

Zoey pulled out her phone, her hand shaking as she read the screen. "Sydney just sent her distress signal!" she yelled.

Dominique rolled her eyes, clearly unimpressed. "Maybe she accidentally got locked in," she remarked, her tone flat.

"Or maybe she's just joking?" Amber asked, her voice low and hesitant. Zoey's temper snapped. She whipped out her phone again, her hand still shaking, and showed them Sydney's distress symbol. A moment later, another text message flashed on the screen, sending a cold shiver down their spines.

"Lucan is after me!" the text message read.
"Would she joke about something like this?" she shouted.
The girls stared at the phone in disbelief. Dominique's and Nia's mouths dropped open, unable to speak. The silence in the room felt suffocating as their eyes flickered between Sydney's distress symbol and the new message. They felt as if they were frozen in place by the cold that touched them. They knew they had to save Sydney, but had no idea how.

CHAPTER 11

The girls sat in intense silence, their minds spinning as they tried to figure out how to save Sydney. None of them looked at each other. The room felt unbearably heavy, as if the air was almost too thick to breathe. Finally, Amber's voice broke through the soundlessness. "Maybe we should call the police?" she murmured, her words hanging in the air.

Nia rolled her eyes, letting out a sharp scoff. "And tell them what?!" she snapped. "That some maniac is trying to turn us into dark fairies, and now, he's after Sydney? They'll think we're insane!"

Dominique quickly turned to face Nia and Amber, her brows almost wrinkling in frustration. "They won't believe us anyway," she said, her voice loaded with anger. "By the time they show up, Sydney's as good as dead."

Zoey paced back and forth, her fingers gripping her skateboard so tightly that her hand turned red. "Well, we can't just sit here," she yelled. "We have to do something!"

Before Zoey could bolt for the door, Dominique grabbed her arm, stopping her in her tracks. "We can't just go out there," she said firmly, her voice full of attitude. "In case you haven't noticed, the school is locked up after hours. No one's *coming* to help us."

Hannah's mind wandered as the others argued around her. Their voices turned into a distant murmur in her ears. She fixed her gaze on Dominique's laptop screen, where another Wikipedia article about fairies and their abilities glowed in the dim light. Her eyes narrowed on one particular ability.

"Hold on," she murmured, lifting her head. "Hey, back up a second," she interrupted, her voice cutting through the conversation. "I wanna try something."

The other girls exchanged puzzled glances at Hannah. Zoey was the first to speak. "Huh? Try what?" she asked.

"Just trust me," Hannah replied, her voice calm but insistent, as if there was no doubt in her mind.

Zoey, Dominique, Amber, and Nia shuffled back reluctantly, giving Hannah space. The living room seemed to hum with the tension that pervaded the area. All eyes were on her. Hannah stared at the TV screen while taking a slow, deep breath, feeling a rush of energy gradually build up in her chest. The air crackled with power, and a faint green glow radiated from her hands, shimmering with a mysterious intensity.

Her necklace pulsed, illuminating in sync with two luminous green orbs that seemed to throb with energy. Slowly, she extended her left hand, her eyes locked on the screen. A swirling green portal materialized before them, revealing glimpses of a dense forest. The room stilled. As the portal shimmered, the green glow in Hannah's eyes faded, returning to their normal dark brown. She stood, faintly quivering, her vision blurring as if the world was spinning around her from the force of magic.

"Ay Dios mío!" Dominique exclaimed.
"Whoa!" Zoey whispered, her voice barely audible.
Nia's eyes expanded, and her mouth dropped open in shock. "How did you do that?" she whispered.

Hannah swallowed hard, trying to regain her composure. "I don't know," she admitted, her words shaking, almost stuttering. "But I remember reading that fairies can teleport to other places."

Dominique's eyes gaped in surprise. "Do you think it can take us to the school?" she asked.

Hannah nodded slowly, her gaze focused on the shimmering portal. "I think so," she murmured, almost to herself.

Without another word, she gradually stepped toward the portal, her foot crossing the threshold. As she did, the candescent green vortex flickered and closed behind her, leaving the girls frozen in place, their eyes riveted with bewilderment. The room was silent, the air laden with tension.

"I'm not … going to like this," Amber whispered, her voice visibly shaky. Twenty minutes passed, and there was still no sign of Hannah. The longer they waited, the more stressful the anxiety in the room, the silence thick and suffocating.

Dominique paced back and forth, grasping her phone tightly. "I'm calling—" she started when Nia interrupted her.

"Relax, just … give her a minute," she said. "She'll come back."
Suddenly, the green portal luminesced back to life, and Hannah stumbled through, breathless but determined. The portal closed behind her with a muted whoosh.

"Well?" Zoey said, impatience written on her face.
Hannah gasped for air, her heartbeat gradually slowing as she caught her breath. "I was right," she said. "The portal led directly to the school. I think if you concentrate hard enough on where you want to go, it will create a path for you."

Amber's expression tightened, her eyes enlarging with doubt and fear. "I … I don't know about this," she stammered, her voice shaky. "This is all so … "

"We don't have a choice, Amber," Zoey said urgently. "Besides, it's the fastest way to get to the school and save Sydney."

Hannah's expression softened, and she placed a reassuring hand on Amber's shoulder. "Zoey's right. We have to do this," she said gently.

Amber averted her attention just a touch away, a knot forming in her stomach. "Listen, Amber," Hannah added, her voice calm but firm. "I know this whole fairy magic thing is scary, but it might help us, too. And it's all we've got. Trust me, we'll be right here with you."

Amber met Hannah's gaze, the sincerity in her eyes sinking in. She took a deep breath, relaxed her shoulders, and a flicker of fortitude crossed her face. "Okay," she whispered, a resolve igniting inside her.

Hannah turned to the others with a confident smile. "All right, now concentrate," she said. The girls nodded, their eyes closed as they listened intently to Hannah's instructions. "Think about the school," Hannah continued.

The girls nodded one at a time, concentrating as they closed their eyes. Green, purple, blue, turquoise, and pink energy filled the room, and their necklaces pulsed with power. With arms outstretched, separate portals began to form, glowing brightly with the strength of their combined magic. Together, they stepped through the shimmering barriers, and in an instant, they stood on the familiar campus of Avalon High.

"We made it," Nia exclaimed, her voice filled with amazement. "We're really here!"

"You're right, Han," Dominique replied with a grin. "Our portals let us travel from one place to another."

Hannah's eyes grew in surprise, and Dominique's words trailed off as she shifted her gaze uncomfortably to the ground. "Uh, I didn't mean to—" she began when Hannah interrupted her with a sweet smile.

"No, it's okay," she said. "I … kinda like my new nickname." Dominique returned the smile, and she let out a deep breath, feeling the tension between them disappear. However, very impatient, Zoey waved her hand, summoning another purple portal with a swift motion.

"Well, what are we waiting for?" she exclaimed, stepping through without hesitation. "Let's get in there, save Sydney, take down this creep, and get out before that security guard shows up again!"

"Girl, wait!" Nia called out, but Zoey was already gone, swallowed by the portal's glow.

Hannah sighed quietly, faintly shaking her head at Zoey's impulsiveness. Her gaze, however, was steady and filled with a calm fearlessness as she locked eyes with Dominique and Nia.

"Come on," she said.
With a shared nod, Dominique and Nia followed her lead. Each focused, created their portals, and stepped through, vanishing into the air. Meanwhile, Lucan and his pack of creatures prowled the halls, their senses sharp, keen eyes scanning every shadow. They were relentlessly closing in on Sydney, and there was nowhere to run. Sydney huddled behind a row of lockers, her breath shallow and stifled as she pressed her hands tightly over her mouth. Her heart pounded in her chest, her mind spinning like a tornado.

One creature growled low, its yellow eyes sweeping the shadows in search of her. Sydney whipped her head back as it drew closer, pressing harder against the cold lockers. Her gaze darted to the ceiling, desperate for a way out. She held her breath, hoping the creature wouldn't hear or notice her. Then, without warning, a warm, orange glow pulsed through her body. Her left hand began to throb, then faded, disappearing before her eyes. Sydney gasped, inhaling shallowly and quickly as she stared in disbelief at her hands, blinking rapidly, trying to understand what was happening.

"What's happening to me?" she questioned, panic rising.
In an instant, her entire body flashed and vanished into thin air. She looked at her invisible hands in shock, a wave of disbelief passing over her. "Whoa," she uttered. "I'm invisible."

There was no time to admire her second power. Sydney's eyes darted across the hallway. Subsequently, her eyes landed on a crumpled soda can on the opposite side of the lockers. Quietly, she snatched it up, holding her breath again. She peered around the lockers, her eyes locking on Lucan and the creatures. They were still circling, still scanning for her.

With precision, Sydney flung the can across the hallway. The metallic clatter bounced off the tiles, ricocheting off the walls. Lucan froze, his eyes snapping toward the sound. His attention shifted, and the surrounding creatures followed suit and rushed toward the noise. In that split second, Sydney took off. Her heart pumped in her chest, heaving as she sprinted toward the stairs.

Lucan's voice echoed behind her, relentless in pursuit. "You can run, but you can't hide!" he bellowed.

Sydney pushed herself harder, racing down the dimly lit hallway. A strange energy surged through her, her body glowing faintly. She barely noticed it until the glow faded, and she could see again, her body no longer invisible. Yet she didn't stop. She charged toward the stairs, determined to escape. Reaching the bottom floor, Sydney lunged toward the front door only to find it locked. She frantically rattled the door handle, pounding her fists against the door. Her breath quickened, labored and uneven.

"Help! Help!" she screamed, her voice desperate enough for someone to hear. "Somebody help me!"

Sydney's cries echoed through the silence, reaching the others. Amber's eyes flared in alarm. "Did you hear that?" she whimpered.

Nia's voice trembled as she resonated with Amber's question. "Is that Sydney?" she asked, her eyes brimming with worry.

Without hesitation, Hannah took off, her adrenaline rushing through her. "Come on!" she commanded, leading Zoey, Dominique, Amber, and Nia in a frantic pursuit to find her.

Sydney's feet hit the floor as she took in sharp gasps. Lucan stepped in front of her, blocking her path. Her heart skipped a beat. A sinister smile spread across his lips as he moved closer, sending her tumbling to the ground with a loud bump.

"You thought your clever trick would work?" he hissed. "There's no one to hear you scream."

Sydney pushed herself off the ground, refusing to show any fear. Her back was straight, even though her hands shook with tension. Her eyes held his, unflinching, cutting through his callous smile.

"Killing me or turning me into your puppet doesn't make you stronger," she spat, her low voice threaded with sharpness. "It makes you a coward—a spineless, weak, pathetic coward who only cares about himself! You hurt others only to please your queen without thinking about anyone else. But you'll never win! You'll lose!"

A rise of fury rushed through Lucan. As he raised his hand, dark tendrils pulsed around him, rising upward from the ground, reaching into the air without disturbing the floor beneath. Sydney felt its cold, suffocating pressure close in on her like an unbearable load. She gasped, struggling to break free, but the darkness tightened, twisting around her in pain and agony.

"You'll think twice before talking to me like that," he snarled.
The dark magic swirled through the air, twisting and warping the space around him. He began a guttural chant in a foreign language, each word loaded with power. It was the same language he and the dark fairies had tried to use on her and the others in the Avalon Forest. Sydney struggled against it, trying to break free by stretching the invisible chains of darkness, but it was no use.

"Now, any last words?" Lucan sneered, his voice thick with malice. Before Sydney could respond, a voice ripped through the air, clear and confident. "Here's one!" it called.

A brilliant pink orb of energy shot through the air, striking Lucan full force and sending him stumbling back. The dark magic holding Sydney in place shattered instantly, releasing her from its grip. As the pressure subsided, she inhaled deeply and felt the tightness leave her chest.

"Leave our friend alone!" Nia cried out, her eyes fierce with perseverance. Lucan turned slowly to Nia, his stunned expression shifting into a cocky smirk. "You really think your weak powers will defeat me?" he scoffed. "You and your pathetic human friends don't have what it takes to be fairies like us."

Nia didn't flinch. She looked him in the eye with a quiet, fierce defiance. The corner of her lip twitched indistinguishably, a subtle sign that she wasn't backing down. Lucan's eyes flickered between her and Sydney, sending a chill down their spines. "Now," he taunted, his voice dripping with malice. "Which one of you will join our beautiful army of dark fairies?"

Then, a blur of motion caught Lucan's eye. His heart skipped, and his smile faltered—Sydney was gone. He jerked his head toward her, already running alongside the others. Nia, avoiding his gaze, followed suit.

Lucan's scream of rage echoed down the hallway, making the air feel cold. Without warning, his wings furiously erupted from his back, his shadow casting over the hallway as he lunged forward, eyes beaming with malevolence. Hannah glanced back and spotted an open classroom door.

"This way!" she shouted, leading the others inside.
The group scrambled into the room, but Lucan was right behind them. Before he could grab the door, Sydney and Nia slammed it shut, trapping his foot in the frame. Without wasting time, Nia stomped hard on Lucan's

foot with her gray, slouchy, knee-high boot. An anguished scream escaped Lucan before he could react.

With their second, desperate push, Sydney and Nia forced the door shut again, their hands bracing against the heavy, polished wood as they strained to keep it closed. For a moment, it seemed like the door would hold, but Lucan's magic pressed back with such force that the door shuddered. Frantically, Zoey, Hannah, Amber, and Dominique quickly piled desks against the door. The barricade held, but the door groaned under the pressure.

"That should hold him," Hannah said, stepping back from the barricade. "Okay, we need a plan," Zoey declared until Dominique's furious outburst interrupted her.

"*We* need a plan?!" she spat. "This is *your* fault!"
Zoey spun around, her eyes sparking with fury as her lips curled into a snarl. "*My* fault?!" she yelled. She stormed toward Dominique, ready to lash out.

"If you hadn't gone to the forest, none of this would've happened!" Dominique raged on, her voice thick with accusation.

"I had to find my necklace!" Zoey retorted. "And if you hadn't convinced us to go to Grilled Cheese Gallery and crashed your car into that restricted area, we wouldn't be in this mess!"

"Guys, can we not argue?" Amber asked, her voice pleading gently.
"Stay out of it!" Zoey and Dominique snapped in unison, their anger flaring together in protest against Amber's attempt to mediate.

Nia quickly jumped in front of Amber, blocking her from the argument. "Hey, don't talk to her like that!" she demanded, her tone fierce but protective. "Calm down!"
Dominique's eyes blazed with fury as she glared at Nia, pushing her back.

"Don't tell me to calm down when I'm not the one losing it!" she shrieked.

"More like dramatic!" Sydney called out, rolling her eyes. "You're not helping!"

Hannah didn't know what to do. She stood frozen, overwhelmed by the chaos surrounding her. Various accusations flew, and guilt crashed over her like a tidal wave, making her feel it was all her fault. She had brought them into this mess by sharing her nightmares, her drawings, and her visions. The room was nothing but shouting and banging, the noise pulling her deeper into a hole of self-blame and regret. Yet through the chaos in her mind, she could still hear Caroline's voice, clear as day. Even after everything, she remembered what her sister used to tell her when they were younger, especially after a thunderstorm: *"Being a leader and a warrior is just as important as being brave."*

Hannah lifted her head slowly, inhaling deeply and releasing a long exhale. Her shoulders relaxed, and a determined spark ignited in her eyes. She knew what she had to do. "Guys, listen," she called out.

Yet the others kept arguing, not even noticing her. Hannah didn't hesitate. She spoke up again, this time with a firm, commanding voice.

"HEY!" she yelled, instantly silencing them.
Filling her chest with air, Hannah began to speak, her voice calm but assertive. The others turned to her, quiet but expectant. "I think I know how to stop Lucan," she said.

Nia raised an eyebrow, clearly doubtful. "How?" she asked.
Hannah's mind raced, recalling when she'd broken free from Lucan's grasp. Her burst of power came out of nowhere—until something clicked.

She remembered stepping on his black zircon amulet, the way it pulsed with strange power. The pieces finally fell into place.

"It's the amulet," she said, her voice filled with sudden clarity. "For some reason, it has some kind of power."

Dominique's eyes magnified. She crossed her arms thoughtfully, tapping the toe of her raffia open-toe buckle ankle strap shoe on the floor. "Which means … it can keep him young," she whispered.

The memory of Lucan's amulet shattering, followed by his sudden aging, vividly flooded Dominique's mind. Suddenly, the dots connected. "That's it!" she said, her voice gaining confidence. "When his necklace broke, he started to age. But if we destroy it completely, he'll … he'll dissolve."

Amber's face lit up with understanding. "Just like the salt dissolving in water in chem class," she said with a grin.

"Exactly," Hannah said, her voice unyielding but reassuring. She gave a steady, purposeful nod. "We need to get the amulet off him."

Nia's face shifted with doubt. She ran her hand through her hair. "But how? He's too strong," she said.

"Yeah, and those creatures won't make it any easier," Zoey agreed, pointing at the door. "We'll never get that amulet."

Sydney placed a steadying hand on Zoey's shoulder, her fingers squeezing. "Well, we'll just have to use our powers," she hushed.

Amber's grin spread wider as she barely bumped her shoulder against Zoey's, her eyes twinkling with mischief. "And teamwork and friendship," she added, her gentle eyes shining with subtle assertiveness.

Zoey smiled back, her eyes blinking to the side before meeting Amber's again. "By the way, I'm sorry I yelled at you," she said.

Dominique walked beside Amber, her smile joining theirs, sending warmth between the three. "Me too," she said mildly.

The tension in the group melted away, and the final traces of hostility disappeared. Amber's expression reflected understanding, and she returned the smile.

"Okay, here's the plan," Hannah conspired, leaning in with a low voice. The girls gathered around, their eyes locked on Hannah, expressions full of steely resolve as they waited for her to share her plan.

Minutes had passed, and Lucan didn't stop, his anger burning with every second. With each blow, he banged on the door with full force, rattling through the walls. Orbs of energy shot from his hands, crashing into the door, but it wouldn't budge.

"I know you're in there!" he roared. "Reveal yourself!"
Inside, the girls took their positions: Hannah stood tall in front of the door, an adamant frown wrinkling her face. She was unshaken, her posture firm and composed, ready to face whatever Lucan would throw at them. Amber crouched behind the teacher's desk as she tried to stifle her shallow breaths. Sydney and Dominique huddled behind the desks in the back row. Zoey and Nia, positioned near the door, exchanged nervous glances. Hannah slowly nodded twice, and Zoey and Nia sprang into action. The two scrambled to push the desks aside, their hands shaking as they quickly cleared a path for her.

"Come on out!" Lucan bellowed, his voice growing louder and more demanding.

Hannah took slow, persistent steps toward the door, each footstep deliberate. Her hand lifted, fingers spread wide in a gesture of surrender. "Okay, I'm coming out!" she said, her voice calm, though it betrayed the tension beneath.

"Han, don't!" Dominique's cries echoed behind her, but Hannah didn't look back, ignoring her completely.

Lucan turned to her, an arrogant smirk playing at the corners of his mouth. "You probably don't want to listen to your pathetic friends," he said.

Hannah's eyes locked with his, unwavering, before slowly facing the others. Sydney gave her a short nod.

"You know," she said, her voice subdued but cold. A dark, icy smile spread across her face as her gaze shifted back to Lucan. "You're right because … I think my plan is going perfectly."

The room fell into stunned silence. The reality of Hannah's words sank in. Sydney's voice broke the quiet, her tone filled with bewilderment. "Plan? What do you mean by 'plan'?" she demanded.

Hannah's lips curved into a playful, mocking smile, her eyes glinting with amusement. "Are you really that clueless?" she scoffed, her voice infused with callousness. "Luring you guys to this stupid school was the best part of my plan. The nightmares, the visions, the 'reason' I moved from Chicago? I just made it all up. I can't believe you actually bought it. You're all so gullible."

Zoey's face twisted in fury, her hands shaking at her side as they clenched into tight fists. She stepped forward, ready to charge toward Hannah, but Nia grabbed her sleeve, pulling her back. "I can't believe this!" she screamed. "You used us!"

Hannah's laugh echoed through the room—cold and cutting, charged with victory.

Sydney took a shaky breath. "When we first met … " she began, her words filled with the pain of betrayal.

"Part of my plan, too," Hannah interrupted, an evil smile forming. Amber's face went pale, her eyes broadening in disbelief as she tried to process what she was hearing. "I don't believe it," she whispered.

"How could you?!" Dominique yelled, barely able to contain her anger.

"We trusted you!" Nia shouted. "You lied to us!"

Hannah's voice rang out, cold and sadistic, slicing through the crushing silence. "Sorry guys, I really did like you guys," she said flatly. "But it was all just for show."

Her words hung in the air, soaked in the treachery of betrayal. The others stood speechless, still reeling from what Hannah had just revealed. Finally, Hannah turned to Lucan, her smile cold and calculating. "I want to join you," she pleaded, deceptively calm. "Make me a dark fairy so I can destroy them."

Lucan studied Hannah, his ominous grin curling like a predator's as he nodded at her request. "If you wish to join me and my beloved mistress, Queen Vivia," he said, his voice dropping to a low, menacing tone. "You must prove your loyalty. Choose one person who will also serve us."

The others exchanged looks, their resolve hardening in their faces. Sydney mouthed, "*Get ready*," her voice barely a whisper.

Hannah's eyes gleamed with malice as she turned toward the group, beginning the ominous chant. "Eeny, meeny, miny, moe, catch a tiger by the toe … " she trailed off, tension thick in the air, until her voice was replaced by a sharp, "You!"

In an instant, Hannah spun around, her hand reaching out to grab Lucan's amulet. He barely had time to react before she snatched it from his neck. With lightning-fast reflexes, Hannah hurled a blinding green orb at him. The impact sent him sprawling to the ground. His face contorted in pain as he let out a guttural groan.

CHAPTER 12

The creatures' eyes glinted with dark hunger as they barreled toward the girls, their growls shaking the air. They moved with lightning speed, claws scraping the floor as the sound of their pursuit rolled through the hallways. The girls had no time to think. One look at the creatures, and they turned to run, hearts racing, their feet banging the floor in a frantic escape.

"Go, go!" Hannah hollered.
Sydney swung the window open, the metal scraping against the frame. The girls climbed through one by one, their bodies slipping through the narrow gap. Nia was last, her foot almost free, when she felt a sharp tug at her leg. Her heart raced. One of the creature's claws wrapped firmly around her ankle, pulling her back toward the dark classroom.

"Help!" Nia cried out, panic creeping into her voice. The others froze, hearing the desperation in her words.

Dominique and Amber rushed back to her, reaching for her hands. They pulled with all their strength, but the creature's claws were massive. Nia gave the creature a fierce glare.

"No!" she wailed. "You mutts are *NOT* taking me back to that psycho!" With all her might, she swung her foot, slamming it into its nose. The creature whimpered in surprise, stumbling back and crashing into another lurking behind it. Without wasting a second, Nia ripped her leg free, delivering one final, powerful kick.

"Come on, come on, come on!" Hannah's voice rang out, sharp and urgent, pushing everyone to hurry. The others pulled Nia further, dragging her the rest of the way through the window.

They hit the ground in the courtyard, gasping for air, their breaths ragged. But before they could recover, more creatures emerged from the shadows, appearing as an army that continued to expand. Their eyes glowed, cruel and hungry, sending a chill down their spines. The air around them thickened, suffocating, as a swarm of dark fairies joined the creatures. Their laughter, evil and frigid, echoed through the cold night, slicing like a blade through the quiet. The girls stumbled backward, their feet crunching on the grass beneath them, their hearts throbbing in their chests. Their eyes were locked on the creatures and the dark fairies, wide with fear, barely able to take in the terrifying sight before them.

Amid the overwhelming tension that enveloped the air, the once familiar sound of the trees rustling seemed far away and largely irrelevant. Then, two more dark fairies swooped down, blocking Amber and Nia's path. Amber jumped back, her heart racing as she stumbled between Sydney and Hannah. Nia's breath quickened as she backed away, quickly scooting between Dominique and Zoey, her body trembling with fear but determined to stay close to her friends.

"Now what?" Sydney asked.
"There are too many of them," Amber said, her voice shaking with fear. The dark fairies and the creatures radiated pure malice, and as they closed in, their evil laughter echoed through the air, chilling them to the core. Just as the nightmare intensified, the clouds parted, revealing a glimpse of the full moon. Its silver light enveloped the forest, casting an elegant glow through the darkness.

"Guys, something's happening!" Zoey exclaimed.
The girls let out a collective gasp as the moonlight touched their necklaces. A stream of energy rippled through the air. Hannah's necklace flared brightly, her aura shimmering in a vivid green. Her wings erupted from her back, glowing brightly as they stretched wide, glittering with power.

Next, Sydney's wings unfurled, glowing with a bold orange light, stretching out confidently. Zoey's wings followed, unfolding in a graceful display of soft purple. Dominique's wings lustered in their blue aura, which glowed like the idyllic ocean. Amber's wings spread out, sharp and cold like the winter breeze. Finally, Nia's wings flared with vibrant pink energy, sparkling with a fierce radiance. At that moment, they went from ordinary girls to fairies again.

"Whoa! I have wings again!" Nia exclaimed, her voice full of awe and disbelief.

"H-how did this happen?" Hannah questioned.
"I remember now," Dominique said, her concentration locked on her wings. "The article mentioned that fairies live in hiding. They might show up during the day but always come out at night. When the full moon rises, their magic gets stronger."

Hannah's eyes beamed, a defiant grin spreading across her face. "Now we know what to do!" she declared.

The girls nodded in silent agreement, their resolve strengthening as the dark fairies closed in. Hannah, still gripping Lucan's amulet, turned to Amber.

"Amber! Catch!" she yelled, tossing the amulet into the air.
Amber's hands fumbled, but she managed to catch it midair just as the dark fairies swarmed closer, their menacing energy filling the space. Hannah hastily summoned her magic. Vines burst from the ground, twisting and wrapping around three dark fairies. The lustrous vines dissolved them into mist with a burst of light. Without wasting a second, Hannah took flight, soaring through the air to catch up with the others as they sped through the forest.

"We can't outrun them forever!" Sydney's voice broke the tense silence. The girls pushed forward, their wings cutting through the air as they fled from the dark fairies and the terrifying creatures chasing them. The wind howled through the forest until Dominique's voice abruptly cut through the noise.

"Look!" she cried, her finger pointing ahead.

The girls followed Dominique's lead and saw it—the same invisible, shimmering wall blocking their path. Hannah's eyes narrowed as a new plan formed in her mind. "Let's lure them to the Avalon Forest!" she exclaimed.

Their wings beat as one, carrying them toward the gleaming barrier with determined expressions on their faces. With a burst of speed, they flew through it and into the depths of the Avalon Forest. As they slowed upon the village, catching their breath, the girls turned to face the dark fairies and the creatures hot on their trail. The fairies stepped out of their homes, confused and unsure of what was happening. Their eyes lifted in panic as they saw the girls, the dark fairies, and the terrifying creatures together. Janessa appeared at the door, her gaze fixed and unafraid, but the mother fairy stood beside her, her face filled with fear. Without warning, she pulled Janessa into a tight hug as if shielding her from the danger closing in.

"Mommy, look!" Janessa shouted, her finger pointing at Hannah. "It's the human girl who saved me!"

The atmosphere grew heavier, thick with tension, as the girls, creatures, and the dark fairies stood face to face. One dark fairy, her eyes burning with malice, caught sight of Amber holding Lucan's amulet.

"Get that amulet!" she shrieked.

Amber met the dark fairy's piercing green gaze, her heart pounding as the fairy's glare sharpened, charging toward her with two others close behind. Staring back with unwavering resolve, Amber turned to Zoey, her voice filled with urgency. "Zoey!" she called out, tossing the amulet to her.

Zoey grabbed the amulet effortlessly, her fingers closing around it as she turned to face the oncoming dark fairies rushing toward her. Amber thrust her hand forward, sending a swirl of glowing orbs hurtling toward them. They burst on impact, splintering into icy shards like broken glass.

Zoey's magic struck next. She flung jagged rocks at the remaining dark fairies and creatures with a powerful motion. They shattered on contact, dissolving into mist. Without hesitation, she summoned a rain of spell orbs, each exploding in bright flashes, disintegrating everything in their wake.

Nia unleashed a furious wind that rippled through the dark fairies like a tornado, tearing them apart. Magic orbs followed, gliding through the atmosphere to finish the remaining enemies. Zoey launched the amulet toward Nia with tremendous aim.

"Nia!" she screamed.
With conviction in her eyes, Nia summoned a powerful gust of wind. The current tore through the dark fairies, scattering them into wisps of smoke. As she soared through the midnight sky, she caught the amulet from the air, her wings slicing through the night with effortless grace.
"Got it!" she yelled, clutching the amulet tightly.
Meanwhile, Dominique fought off the last dark fairies, her movements sharp and desperate. One of them raised a hand, dark magic swirling around it as it lunged toward her. Dominique barely had time to step back before she found herself drawn to the moonlit lake nearby. With a blast of magic, she unleashed a crashing wave that swept the fairy and the others into the water with a strong splash.

"Dominique!" Nia's voice called out.
Nia threw the amulet with precision, and Dominique spun around, her heart racing. She caught it just as another dark fairy swooped down, missing her by an inch. Her gaze flickered to Sydney, and she shouted her name. Dominique tossed the amulet toward her with a flick of her wrist. Arriving just in time, Sydney snatched it out of the air with flawless accuracy.

Sydney didn't hesitate. With a fierce wave of her hand, a flood of spell orbs and fire blasts exploded from her, tearing through the air and reducing the remaining dark fairies into ashes. The girls paused, catching their breath, eyes scanning around the village. As the smoke cleared, it hit them: No more dark fairies or creatures were there. But then their gaze lifted. The fairies had been watching from the shadows the entire time, their eyes glinting in the distance.

Before they could celebrate, a bone-chilling roar cut through Sydney's ears. "Enough!" Lucan's voice resounded through the forest, laced with rage.

"Watch out!" she screamed.
The girls scattered, scarcely dodging the destructive wave of energy that shot toward them. Lucan stood tall, his wings tense with a fury he struggled to contain. His chest heaved as his blazing eyes locked onto the girls, anger palpable in the thick air. The fairies scrambled back to their homes, including the mother fairy, who hurriedly pulled Janessa away.

"I've had enough of this!" Lucan snarled, his teeth gritted, his voice dripping with fury. "This ends here and now."

The girls stood tall, fearless, their resolve fiercer than ever. They were ready to face Lucan head-on. With his deluge of crackling dark energy, Lucan charged at them again. However, Hannah's voice, direct and commanding, rang out before he could reach them.

"Now!" she shouted.
Hannah, Sydney, Zoey, Dominique, and Amber soared into the sky, leaving Nia behind. In an instant, Nia vanished, replaced by a swirling vortex of wind. It roared, encircling Lucan like a powerful whirlpool, trapping him within its fury. Lucan's eyes flared as he struggled against the winds, sending a barrage of spell orbs. Thankfully, Nia's glowing pink force field effortlessly deflected them all in a blur. In the chaos, Zoey grinned, her eyes sparkling with mischief. She hurled a purple spell orb that struck Lucan's hand with a loud crack. He turned toward her, fury

bubbling to the surface, his eyes burning with madness.

"Come and get me, creep," she taunted, her voice steeped with daring and excitement.

Lucan's anger boiled even more. His lips curved into a snarl as he charged after her.

"It's working! Keep going!" Hannah shouted.
Focused on Zoey, Lucan didn't see Dominique coming. With a swift wave of her hands, she unleashed a massive blast of water that slammed into him, sending him crashing backward. Stunned, Lucan looked around, confused. He was all alone.

Sneaking up from behind, Sydney struck him with a wave of fire that licked at his skin.

Amber didn't hesitate. A sharp projectile shot from her hands, freezing part of his face in an instant. Lucan howled in pain, the ice cracking as his fury reached a boiling point. His head whipped toward Hannah, who stood boldly in front of him. A cruel, mocking sneer spread across his lips.

"You honestly think you can fool me?" he jeered, his words dripping with contempt. "You don't have what it takes to be a fairy—no knowledge, no power! You don't belong here. You never did! And now, you and your worthless friends … will meet your end!"

Hannah's necklace emitted a faint green light, reflecting the moonlight's glow and casting eerie shadows across the ground. She stole a glance at the others, then locked her gaze back on Lucan, her eyes unwavering as she spoke in a low but fierce voice.

"You're right about one thing," she stated. "I don't know anything about being a fairy."

As she spoke, her eyes shone a fierce green. Her hand pulsed with magic, and vines erupted from the ground, twisting around Lucan's limbs, holding him securely. Hannah kept her other hand hidden behind her back, clutching something small, her grip firm.

"But we're not afraid of you anymore," she finished, her voice more emphatic and bolder. "Because…we're the ones who will end your reign of terror."

Lucan's desperate scream didn't stop Hannah. With a swift motion, she hurled the object she had hidden—Lucan's amulet—toward a nearby tree. It crashed into the trunk, shattering on impact, scattering glowing shards across the ground. Lucan let out a scream of disbelief, his face twisting in agony. Pain rippled through him as his body aged instantaneously, crumbling into dust, the ashes swept away by the wind. Hannah's hand and eyes tremored, the green glow fading, and a wave of exhaustion hit her like a crashing wave, dragging her down. Her wings fluttered weakly, barely able to keep her afloat. She swayed and would've collapsed if not for Sydney, who caught her just in time.

 "Your plan worked, Hannah!" Sydney exclaimed. "You did it."
Hannah managed a faint, tired smile, shaking her head gently. "No, we did it," she declared, just loud enough to hear.

At that moment, without thinking, Hannah pulled Sydney into a hug. The burden of everything that had happened—from their new powers to becoming fairies and their first victory—melted away in that embrace. The battle was over, and they were safe. Together, they had stopped Lucan, the dark fairies, and the creatures.

Sydney hugged her back, a smile spreading across her face. "We really did," she said, feeling the bond of their friendship tighter than ever.

The other girls gathered around them, sharing in the victory. Zoey, Dominique, Amber, and Nia joined in, wrapping them all in a group hug, their smiles brighter than the moonlit sky above—all thanks to Hannah's plan. Dominique broke the silence, her eyes fluttering as she grinned.

"Let's get out of here," she laughed.
The others nodded, giggling and laughing along with her, the tension of the battle melting away. Their wings illuminated in the cool night air as they passed through the invisible barrier, returning to their world. As they landed in the school courtyard, their wings glowed fleetingly before fading into specks of light, the magic slipping away as swiftly as it had appeared.

Sydney's hand tightened around her keys as she slung her orange soccer backpack—the ball bulging from its compartment into the back of her car. "I guess I'll see you guys next week," she said, her voice light but a little tired from the night's events.

Just as Sydney was about to slide into the driver's seat, Hannah stopped midway, her hand resting casually on the car door. "Wait," she said, her eyes twinkling with zeal. "I think I found an easier way for you to get home."

Sydney raised an eyebrow and tilted her head, her curiosity piqued. "What do you mean?" she asked.

Hannah's grin overtook her face. She took a deep breath, her green aura flaring to life around her like a spark of energy. A glowing, swirling portal glistened into existence before them, offering glimpses of Sydney's house.

Sydney gasped, her mouth hanging open. "Whoa!" she said, her eyes colossal in disbelief. "How did you do that?"

Hannah's sly smile grew. She tilted her head a bit, her eyes alive with mischief. She shot a rascally grin at the others before turning back to Sydney. "Let's just say … we discovered that fairies can do more than fly and use powers," she said.

Their giggles bubbled up, ringing through the air. Sydney pulled Hannah into a quick hug, her joy contagious. "You guys are seriously amazing," she said, her voice bright with wonder.

After the hug, Sydney waved at the others before slipping into her car. The engine roared to life, and she drove right into the portal, disappearing just before it vanished.

As the portal flickered out of existence, Hannah, Zoey, Dominique, Amber, and Nia looked around, ensuring the coast was clear. A faint ripple of energy pulsed through the air, and with a gush of magic, they were instantly transported back to Hannah's house. The colorful portals closed behind them, one by one, like doors quietly shutting. Nia turned to Zoey, a grin forming across her face.

"Want a ride?" she asked. "I can take you home if you want."
Zoey's exhausted eyes lit up with gratitude. "Sure," she said, the corners of her lips forming a gracious smile. "I don't wanna ride my board alone at night anyway."

After gathering their belongings and saying their goodbyes, Nia, Dominique, Amber, and Zoey piled into Nia's Jeep. Hannah watched as they drove off, the engine's hum fading in the distance. She lingered on the doorstep for a second, releasing a quick sigh of relief before stepping inside. As the door clicked inaudibly behind her, her parents' muffled laughter drifted from the kitchen.

"Hey, I didn't know you were in the living room," Jeremy called out.
"Sorry, uh … my friends and I were … doing some math homework," Hannah stammered, her cheeks flushing.

As she climbed the stairs, a strange wave of emotions washed over her. It was like a secret she'd been hiding suddenly surfaced. She realized she had been keeping her true feelings about Avalon buried all along, held back by the memories of Caroline. Just as she turned back toward the kitchen, she caught her mom's watchful observation. Maggie watched her, a quiet look of concern written in her eyes.

"Sweetie?" she inquired gently. "Is something wrong?"
Hannah drew a cleansing breath, feeling her heart accelerate in her chest. The fluttering in her stomach slowly faded, but her hands still trembled a little. She swallowed hard, trying to regain her composure. "Actually, I've been thinking," she began, her voice shaky. "Even though I miss Chicago … and Caroline, I feel like Avalon is starting to feel like a second home. I think I'm ready to give it another shot."

Her parents' faces lit up in surprise, then melted into smiles of relief and happiness. Hannah felt their sensitivity radiate through her as the burden that had been bearing on her shoulders lifted—the silence breaking away. She stepped closer to her mom, who immediately opened her arms, pulling her into a tight hug and kissing her forehead.

Just then, Sadie rushed into the room, her energy bursting down the stairs. She flung herself into their dad's arms, hugging him with all her might. Her contagious enthusiasm made Hannah's heart skip a beat. She looked at her, and the two couldn't help but giggle at their parents' happy faces.

"Do you think … I could invite my friends over again sometime?" Hannah asked.

"Sure," Jeremy replied, his low voice kind and soothing. "Whenever you want."

Hannah smiled lovingly at her dad's response, her eyes lighting up. Maggie, standing beside her, gave her a playful nudge. "See? I told you that you'd like it here," she spouted. "You just needed to give it a chance."

The simple words from her mom made Hannah's heart soar. She glanced over at Sadie, who was eager for her turn.

"Uh … do I get to invite my friends, too?" Sadie asked, her voice full of childlike curiosity.

Laughter filled the room, and the sound of it wrapped around them like a cozy blanket. Hannah took in the moment, feeling the affection of her family's love. For the first time since leaving Chicago, she knew she'd found her place—not just because of her family, but because of her new friends, too.

The next day, at her parents' request, Hannah invited Sydney, Zoey, Dominique, Amber, and Nia over for the weekend. She gave them a real, proper tour of the house, proudly showing them everything—from the living room to the kitchen. Her parents, although distant at first, seemed to warm up, their voices blending with the chatter and laughter of the girls. Even Sadie smiled and made conversation, zealously getting to know the group. As Hannah opened her bedroom door, she and the others whispered animatedly about Sydney discovering the ability to turn invisible.

Nia's eyes grew in size. "Wait, hold up," she said. "You can *turn invisible?* Girl, how'd you do that?"

Sydney shrugged. "I don't know … It just happened," she said, lowering her voice as she struggled to wrap her mind around the invisibility power. "I was in the hallway, trying to get away from Lucan and those creatures, and then … I got cornered."

She looked down, still in disbelief, before turning to the others. "I didn't know what else to do … until I felt this orange glow pulsing through my body," she continued. "At first, it was just my hand throbbing, but then … it started to fade. Like, it disappeared before my eyes, and when I looked at the rest of me, I was completely gone—invisible."

Amber gasped inconspicuously. "That's … kind of amazing," she said, leaning forward.

Sydney nodded, her eyes unfocused as the memory replayed. "I couldn't believe it at first either," she said. "I still felt everything, but I couldn't see myself, not even my hands."

Zoey's grin spread as she crossed her arms. "Okay, now that's just straight-up superhero vibes," she shouted. "That's epic!"

The others shushed her. Zoey giggled and quickly muttered, "Sorry," in an undertone.

Sydney nodded, her eyes still vast, as if the memory was playing in her mind. "It definitely felt like superpowers," she said, almost to herself. "Then, I realized I had to act fast. So, I threw a soda can as a distraction to buy me some time, but it didn't go as planned."

Dominique, who had listened attentively, grinned as her eyes lit up. "One of the fairies' abilities is turning invisible," she announced.

Sydney's brow furrowed in surprise and curiosity. "You guys read about that?" she investigated, her voice tinged with disbelief.

Dominique nodded, her head almost tilting undetectably. "We … read more about fairies and their abilities," she explained.

Before anyone else could respond, their attention shifted toward Hannah's bedroom. The door creaked open, and they all stepped inside, their eyes enlarging dramatically as they took in the sight of it, including her drawings.

"This is your room?" Amber asked, her eyes grew expansive with awe. Hannah smiled shyly. "Yeah, it's not big, but—" she replied when Dominique interrupted her.

"It's cute," she said, a smile spreading across her lips. "Kind of like my room, but yours is way prettier."

Hannah returned Dominique's smile. "Thanks," Hannah said, feeling a little brighter inside. "I think our rooms are both cute."

Zoey studied Hannah's drawings, her eyes growing gigantic in surprise. "Wow, Hannah! You drew all these?" she asked with admiration.

Hannah let out a small laugh, feeling her nerves melt away. "Yep," she replied. "I drew them when I was five."

"No wonder you're so talented!" Zoey exclaimed. "I mean, it's cool and all, but my graffiti's got the edge."

"Yeah, they're amazing," Sydney added, clearly intrigued.
"At least you don't have the drawing of Lucan," Nia laughed.
"No way, I'd never do that—never in a million years," Hannah chuckled at Nia's joke.

The girls burst into laughter, their voices echoing through the room. Hannah closed the door, her smile dimming bit by bit as she exhaled. She glanced at her friends and then spoke. Her quiet voice was serious but genuine. "Speaking of that," she began. "I want to say thank you."

"For what?" asked a puzzled Amber, angling her head slightly as her brow wrinkled in confusion.

Hannah took another long inhale, her hand fidgeting with the sleeve of her ombre yellow, long-sleeved T-shirt as she spoke. "For believing in me, listening to me, and supporting me," she said. "I've realized now that moving to Avalon, transferring to Avalon High, and meeting you guys was the best thing that ever happened to me. It's even helped me move on from … my sister's disappearance … "

Sydney, Zoey, Dominique, Amber, and Nia exchanged quiet glances, their faces displaying sympathy as they watched Hannah. The significance of her words lingered in the air, thick with emotion. For a brief moment, no one spoke. Finally, Hannah looked up, her expression shifting as her tone changed.

"Anyway, um … to show my gratitude to all of you, I got you guys something," Hannah said, opening her dresser drawer.

Hannah pulled out six small magnetic gift boxes, each wrapped in colorful organza ribbons: orange, purple, blue, turquoise, and pink. One by one, she handed them out, starting with Sydney. "This one's for you," she said, giving her the orange box.

Next, she passed the purple box to Zoey. "For you," she added with a smile.

The blue box went to Dominique, followed by the turquoise one for Amber. Finally, Hannah handed Nia the pink box with a grin.

"Your favorite color!" she sang.
Sydney, Zoey, Dominique, and Amber thanked Hannah while Nia cheerfully sang, "My favorite color!" before eagerly opening her box.

Nia let out a surprised gasp as she pulled out a silver and pink chain-link charm bracelet. Each charm on the bracelet, a tiny silver link engraved with one of their names, gleamed in the afternoon sunlight. Nia's eyes grew round as she read her name, her fingers lightly brushing over the smooth, shiny surface.

"Oh, Hannah … this is amazing," she gasped.
The others leaned in, mesmerized by the beauty of their own bracelets. Each was the same style as Nia's—all with the same chain-link style but with uniquely suited color combinations for each girl.

Sydney's was a bold mix of silver and orange, the orange glistening like a sunset. Zoey's was silver and purple. Its rich color matched the night sky.

Dominique's was silver and blue, evoking the peacefulness of the sea. Amber's was silver and turquoise, a bright, energetic combination like crystalline ice.

 A chorus of gasps and exclamations filled the room as the girls marveled at the personal touch of their bracelets. Each one felt unique to them, as if the charms were a tiny representation of their personality.

"Wait, what about yours?" Dominique asked, her eyes sparkling with curiosity as she glanced at Hannah's seemingly empty wrist.

With a sly smile, Hannah pulled down her sleeve, revealing her bracelet—a silver and green combination corresponding with the spring leaves. "I don't know if I picked the right colors for you guys," she said. "These were the only colors they had left. And I know Nia's favorite color is pink, and green's my favorite."

"Actually, orange *is* my favorite color," Sydney laughed, brushing a strand of her hair behind her ear.

Zoey chuckled, winking at Hannah. "I'd say you scored a point because purple's my favorite," she replied with a grin.

Dominique chimed in, her fingers brushing the sleeve of her purple cold-shoulder blouse. "Blue's my favorite," she said.

"And I love turquoise," Amber added sheepishly, her voice barely above a whisper.

Hannah smiled fondly, leaning closer to Sydney and Amber as she sat on the bed. "Thanks, guys," she said.

"You know," Zoey said, leaning forward with a mischievous grin spreading across her face. "We should come up with a team name. I was thinking maybe *The Gladiators* or *The Dominators?*"

She continues to toss out more ideas, each sillier than the last. The others exchanged confused glances, their patience starting to run thin.

Zoey's eyes lit up as she clapped her hands together. "Oh wait! Wait! Wait! Wait! How about … the *Powerhousers?*" Zoey cheerfully exclaimed. "You know, because we totally kicked Lucan's butt."

Nia scoffed, rolling her eyes. "Girl, that is *so* cheesy," she laughed. "Why would we ever call ourselves that?"

Dominique sighed dramatically, straightening up. "I'd say we should be the *Intellect Trendsetters,*" she said, her voice decisive. "It's elegant, and it reflects our strength."

Sydney scoffed, nudging Dominique's shoulder. "Come on, Dom, that's boring," she teased with a grin. "We should be the *Cool Mavericks.*"

"What about the *Synergy Weavers?*" Amber shyly asked, her soft voice laced with hesitation.

Nia shook her head. "We should be the *Electric Sisterhood,*" she said assertively.

The girls glanced at each other, then shook their heads in unison before bursting into giggles. "No," they said together.

Sydney turned toward Hannah. "What do you think we should be, Hannah?" she asked, her brow arched in curiosity. "Got any ideas?"

Hannah turned toward her dresser and pulled open the bottom drawer. "Actually," she said, "I thought about it for a while last night, and I think I came up with the perfect name." She flipped open her sketchbook, revealing the words *Mystic Pact* written in bold, black letters.

Dominique raised an eyebrow. "*The Mystic Pact?* I like it," she said gleefully. "The Mystic Pact's pretty cool!" Zoey interjected, her grin expansive as she gave Hannah an approving nod. "You nailed it."

"That's fabulous! It totally fits us!" Sydney said.
"The Mystic Pact has my vote!" said Nia, nodding approvingly at Hannah.

"I love it!" Amber said with a shy smile.

Hannah erupted into laughter, feeling a wave of relief. "Then, it's official," she said, holding her hand. "We are the Mystic Pact."

The girls joined in one by one, stacking their hands on each other. Together, they cheered, "We're the Mystic Pact! Where magic and friendship come to life!"

"I LOVE IT," Hannah said happily.
The girls laughed, cheering and high-fiving each other, their exuberance filling the room. Suddenly, the door creaked open, and Sadie poked her head in. "Hey, uh … Mom and Dad said dinner is about to be ready," she said, her body shifting awkwardly in the doorway. "They were wondering if you guys want to stay?"

The girls exchanged looks, each one pondering a decision. After a brief moment of silence, Hannah spoke up. "Do you guys want to—" she started before Sydney beat her to it.

"I'm cool with staying over," she said, shrugging her shoulders as she grinned.

"Oh yeah, most definitely," Dominique added.
"Yeah, I can eat. I'm starving," Nia said, nodding eagerly.
Amber and Zoey exchanged a look of agreement, their smiles radiating as big as ever.

Hannah turned to Sadie, a tiny smile on her face as her brow pinched in curiosity. "By the way, what are we having?" she asked.

"Salisbury steak, baked ravioli, and asparagus," Sadie replied with a mischievous smile before closing the door behind her.

The girls turned to Hannah, knowing that her parents were excellent cooks. Their brows knitted together, wondering what they were like outside the kitchen. Hannah let out a suppressed chuckle.

"Okay, I can eat a ton of veggies, but asparagus … not so much," joked Hannah.

The girls laughed spiritedly at Hannah's joke, but Sydney's smile faded gradually, her eyes distant as her mind lingered on something. "So, what do you think happened to that Queen Vivia?" she asked, her voice ringing with curiosity.

Hannah shrugged. "Well, wherever she is," she said calmly. "Let's hope we don't run into her again."

"Or talk to her," Zoey added, her expression almost darkening. "She's worse than Heather and her goons."

"That's for sure," Nia agreed. "I don't even wanna cross paths with her again."

"I'm pretty sure the police have no clue where she and those dark fairies and creatures came from," Amber joined in, shaking her head in agreement.

"No doubt," Dominique said. "They probably wouldn't believe it even if we told them."

The girls were right about one thing: they couldn't shake the feeling that Queen Vivia might return. If she did, it would be with a vengeance—whether because of Lucan's death or interfering with her plans to destroy the Avalon Forest. They also couldn't ignore that Avalon held more secrets than just being a realm of fairies.

For now, though, they pushed those thoughts aside. They were still getting to know each other by discovering the meaning behind their shared necklaces, each with a unique birthstone and zodiac sign. They wanted to learn to work together, harness their new powers, and grow closer as friends. Their bond had strengthened with every step, and their magic and friendship had miraculously come to life through it all!

THANKS FOR READING BOOK 1:

Into the Avalon Forest!
Stay tuned for The Mystic Pact's next adventure and unlock more

secrets in Book 2:

Unleash the Sprites

Amber's house
Sydney's house
Hannah's house
Open Air Mall
Nia's house
Zoey's house
Dominique's house
High School
Avalon

— sparkling areas
— dark fairy clan
— invisible wall
Home to Queen Vivia
The Fairy World

ABOUT THE AUTHOR

M'Sharra Peters

Born on January 23rd and raised in Kansas City, Missouri, M'Sharra Peters is a creative Aquarian that is passionate about storytelling stemming from a wild imagination. She began writing at the age of six as a way to express herself and has been crafting stories ever since. In 2020, she moved to Texas and earned her B.A. in English with a concentration in Creative Writing and is currently working toward her Master's in English with a certificate in Creative Writing.

Known for being kind, creative, funny, and adventurous – though a bit shy at first, she enjoys opening up through writing and many creative pursuits.

Her debut novel, ***Into the Avalon Forest***, is the first in Secrets in Avalon, a planned 28-book series blending fantasy, mystery, adventure, and coming-of-age themes.

This children's and young adult fantasy adventure blends mystery, magic, and coming-of-age themes, aimed at readers from 5th to 12th grade.

Inspired by her own experiences and beloved nostalgic shows, books, movies, computer games, video games, and her love for books, as well as strong characters, including female characters, she aims to write stories to give a voice to young girls navigating the challenges of growing up as a reminder that they deserve to be the heroes of their own stories, especially throughout friendship and challenges. When she's not writing, M'Sharra enjoys listening to music, singing, audio engineering, taking selfies, traveling, dancing, and fashion. She's also a former soccer player who's carried the lessons of teamwork, friendship, challenges, and perseverance into her creative journey. She has also enjoyed horseback riding as a 4H and saddle club member as well as performing live shows as a member of School of Rock. She proudly embraces her inner shopaholic spirit.